NO DIRECTION HOME

EASTWOOD

BOOK 2

MIKE SHERIDAN

Editing by Felicia Sullivan

Proofreading by Laurel Kriegler

Cover art by Deranged Doctor Design

Also by Mike Sheridan

WINTER'S EDGE
(Book 1 of the Outzone Drifter series)

GRAYFALL
(Book 2 of the Outzone Drifter series)

OUTZONE RAIDER
(a stand-alone novel)

CHAPTER 1

On a residential back street in Old Fort, Tennessee, the next town south of Ocoee, Mason Bonner and Russ Willis sat in the front garden of a large corner house. Though the lawn was in need of mowing, the garden still looked good. Bright orange anemones and catmint lined either side of the center walkway leading to the front porch, and in one corner was a paved courtyard, where the two men sat at an expensive-looking patio table.

Give it another month, this will have all turned to jungle, Mason thought to himself idly. *Just like the rest of the world.*

That morning, he and his crew had made the two hour trip from Knoxville in a combination of motorhomes, campervans, and trailers. Over the past couple of days, he'd worked hard preparing for the move, stocking up on as much food, guns, ammunition, gasoline, and medical supplies as he could. Once he left the city, there would be no going back.

Russ had rendezvoused with the group in downtown Cleveland, where he'd guided the convoy along the back roads to Old Fort, lessening the chance they would be spotted in the area. With such a large gang, it was best no one got wind of Mason's arrival.

He leaned over the table, studying a local map Russ had brought with him. It was his first chance to examine the area in detail. Along with Russ's sketch of Wasson Lodge, it gave him a better idea of what he was up against. Later that day, he would drive up and get a firsthand view for himself.

The YMCA camp was closer to the lodge than he had previously imagined. The properties were set on either side of a large headland that jutted out into Lake Ocoee, and Russ informed him that the two camps were in constant communication with each other. Once Mason took over the lodge, they would make uneasy neighbors.

That meant only one thing.

On the map, Russ had marked the positions of the two roadblocks on the Cookson Creek Road.

"How often do people come in and out of the camp?" he asked.

"Every day," Russ told him. "They're still collecting supplies as far as I can tell."

Mason let out a satisfied grunt. "Good." He took the pen out of Russ's hand and jabbed the ballpoint at a spot farther west, where the Cookson Creek Road intersected with Sloans Gap Road. "If anyone goes to Cleveland or Chattanooga, they need to come this way, I'm guessing."

Russ nodded. "It's the most direct route to the 411."

Mason made a mark across the road, similar to the ones Russ had made on the Cookson Creek Road. "Somewhere here, we're going to set up our own position. An ambush point. We'll pick off anyone leaving the YMCA camp, see if we can't whittle down their numbers a little." He grinned at Russ. "I run a big crew, we need space. After we take the lodge, I plan on taking here next."

Russ's eyes lit up. "Great idea! They never leave camp without at least three people in a vehicle, so we'll get a few of them for sure. This afternoon I'll scout out the best place to set up the ambush." His eyes narrowed. "When do we take the lodge, Mason?"

"Tomorrow night. We'll attack at four in the morning, when they least expect it." An unpleasant smile came to Mason's lips. "This is going to be Walter's worst nightmare. I can't wait to see his face when he sees us."

Russ hesitated a moment before answering. "Uh, Mason…Walter left the lodge yesterday afternoon. He was towing his trailer, so I think he's left for good. Pete and the young kid went with him. I recognized their pickups."

Mason frowned. "Where the hell did they go?"

There was another hesitation. "That's the thing. I'm not sure."

"Why not? Didn't you follow them?"

"Of course. Problem is, I lost them. I had to drive the long way around the roadblock so I wouldn't get spotted. By the time I got back onto Cookson, they'd disappeared."

Mason's face darkened. "You couldn't catch up with them on your motorbike?"

Russ shook his head. "You don't understand. I drove all the way back to the highway without coming across them. They must have headed south, not west, otherwise I'd have caught up with them for sure." He smiled nervously. "Good news is, it means we should find them pretty quick when we want to."

Mason stared at Russ, trying to figure out whether he was lying or not just to save his ass. "Why do you say that?"

Russ pointed back down at the map and traced a finger along the Cookson Creek Road. "South heads deeper into the Cohutta," he explained. "There's nothing there but forest. They must plan on staying in the area."

Studying the map again, Mason took his point. The Cookson Road followed Lake Ocoee's southern shore deeper into the forest. It made no sense for Walter to go that way unless he planned on staying in the area.

"All right," he said finally. "For the moment, looks like Walter's got a reprieve." He scowled at Russ. "Not for long, though. He'll be dead meat soon enough. That goes for Pete and the boy too. I'll make them pay for what they did. Big time."

CHAPTER 2

At Wasson Lodge, the remnants of the Camp Knox survivors group convened in the living room for their daily brief. Five strained faces stared anxiously at their leader, a far cry from the nine that had sat cheerfully around him only the previous day.

Chris had barely slept. The entire night he had replayed over and over in his mind the events leading to the exodus of five members of his fledgling community, as well as the three new arrivals from Atlanta. Led by Walter, they had gone off to form their own group, one that was now larger than his own.

The turn of events had stunned him. A combination of bad luck, and if he was to admit it, bad judgment, had defeated him. He had allowed his anger over Emma's involvement with Cody to cloud his reasoning, and it had been his fracas with the youngster that had sparked the whole thing off.

He had been unlucky in his fight with Walter, however, where he'd been knocked out by a lucky punch. It still hurt like hell. Not the punch—he'd quickly recovered from that—it was his bruised ego that would take longer to heal.

He looked around at the five glum faces, and knew he had to turn this thing around fast or else others might choose to leave and join Walter's group. In a situation like this, things could change quickly.

"All right, people," he began in a calm, measured voice. "Yesterday was not the best of days. No point in pretending otherwise. While I never felt comfortable with Walter or his two friends, for that matter, losing Greta and Emma is a setback." He leaned forward in his seat and gazed around the room, looking each person in the eye. "But this is a survival situation. We just have to get on with it. We have a great camp with excellent facilities. We're not going to have any problems finding other survivors to join us. Right now, though, the most important thing is security. We need to make sure we hold onto this place."

Sitting next to him, Liz spoke up. "Chris, that's going to be hard. There's simply not enough of us to keep a constant guard." There was a look of real concern on her face. Staring at her closer, Chris realized it was more than that. She was scared. "All I hear about is the gangs. It sounds like they're everywhere now."

What she said was true. And with only six of them to defend such a prize possession as the lodge, the camp would be vulnerable to attack. Many of the gangs that roved the lakeside were more than fifteen-strong.

"In the next few days, we'll bolster our numbers back to where we were before, perhaps even more," Chris reassured her. "And once we finish work on the perimeter fence, no one is going to bother us."

Liz's eyes wavered uncertainly. "Are you sure we'll find more people?"

"Absolutely. Anyone traveling on their own will be desperate to come to a place like this, a sanctuary with civilized people. Remember, they'll be lonely and afraid. Some will have run into trouble already. That's going to make them even more keen to join us." He smiled. "Stay strong, Liz. This is all going to work out, trust me."

On the coffee table in front of him, the radio crackled to life. *"Chris, this is Sheriff Rollins. Do you read me? Over."*

Chris hesitated. This was a conversation he'd prefer to have in private. Nonetheless, it might appear weak if he ignored Rollins or switched the radio off. Reaching over, he picked up the handset and pressed the Talk button. "Read you loud and clear, Sheriff. What can I do for you, over?"

"I've been informed that there's been a change of situation at your camp. We need to meet right away to discuss it, over."

"Sheriff, everything is fine here. Right now I'm busy. I'll contact you later in the day, over."

"Chris, your change in status impacts us here too," Rollins replied curtly. *"I'll be over within the hour. Over and out."*

Trying not to show any visible signs of annoyance, Chris put the handset back down on the table. He composed himself and stared down at his notes.

"All right, let's discuss camp security. We're over halfway done with the perimeter fence. No reason why we can't have it finished in the next couple of days. Eddy, what's the status? Do we need to make another run into Cleveland today for supplies?"

As his security chief began his update, Chris's mind wandered back to something he'd sworn to himself before finally dropping off to sleep the previous night. When Camp Knox was back up to full strength, he'd set about getting his revenge on Walter. He'd take care of Cody too while he was at it. What that revenge would be, he wasn't sure yet, but Chris wasn't a man who took defeat lightly. It would be something…*substantial.*

CHAPTER 3

Late morning, a silver Nissan Frontier pulled off Route 411 and into the town of Benton, Tennessee. Inside the vehicle was Jonah Murphy, his wife Colleen, and their new friend, Monica Jeffreys. Weaving through the back streets, the Nissan turned onto Station Road and parked outside the First Volunteer Bank.

"All right, now what?" Jonah said, peering through the windscreen at the deserted streets.

The previous day, he and Colleen had come across a gang of men in the process of assaulting Monica outside a supermarket in Richmond Hill, Savannah. Thanks to some scary driving on Jonah's part, combined with some deft sharpshooting on Colleen's, the couple had saved Monica and journeyed on toward Benton, the town she was from.

On the way, they'd stopped in downtown Chattanooga. Monica needed to restock on everything she'd lost back in Richmond. By the time they left the city, it was approaching dusk. In a small wood on the outskirts of town, they'd driven up a forest track and set up camp for the night. That morning, after a quick breakfast of instant coffee and dry biscuits, they'd packed up and made the final leg of their journey to Benton.

In the back seat, Monica peered out her window. "There's no sign of activity. It doesn't look like there's a single soul here."

Behind the wheel, Jonah shrugged. "Dead as a dodo. Same as every other town we've passed through."

"I know," Monica replied worriedly. "It's just that, now we're here, I don't really know what to do. You don't think everyone is dead, do you?"

Sitting in the front passenger seat, one hand gripped on the barrel of her M-15 Armalite rifle, Colleen shook her head. "Impossible. From everything I learned before the Internet went down, the virus has roughly a two percent survival rate. Who knows how many more managed to avoid it? No reason why Benton should be any different. You say the population here was around fifteen hundred?" Monica nodded. "That means there should be at least thirty survivors." She turned in her seat to face Monica. "They've obviously gone somewhere. Any idea where?"

Monica thought for a moment. "I suppose they may have gone to one of the farms outside town, or maybe up to the lake."

"All right, let's see if we can find them. Jonah, start the car."

"Okay, boss." Jonah turned the ignition key and the engine coughed smoothly to life. He looked up at the rearview mirror. "Which way, Monica?"

Monica pointed left. "Let's head east out of town. That's where most of the farms are. It's our best bet."

Jonah shifted the gear selector into drive and pulled out onto the street. He drove no more than twenty yards before coming to an abrupt stop again. "You know what?" he said, looking over at his wife. "Maybe there's no need to go searching for anyone."

Colleen frowned. "Why is that?"

Jonah glanced in his side mirror where an olive-green Mitsubishi Pajero had come to a stop fifty yards behind them.

"Because we got company, that's why. With a bit of luck, it's someone from around here."

Colleen swiveled in her seat and stared out the rear window. Immediately, she pulled her Glock 21 out of her holster and handed it to Monica. "You know how to use one of these?"

Monica nodded, taking the weapon.

All three got out of the car, Colleen armed with her M-15, Jonah and Monica with their .45 pistols. Behind them, three heavily-armed men did likewise and stood behind their vehicle, which they'd parked lengthways across the street.

One of them, a big burly man with a thick beard and a protruding belly, called out to them gruffly. "Hey, what are you people doing in our town?" He wore plaid flannels and overalls, and looked like he was about to go off to work cutting down trees in the forest. All he was short of was the axe, Jonah thought.

He was about to reply when Monica stepped away from the Nissan toward the man. She stared intently at him as she got closer. "Bert...is that you?"

Lowering his rifle, the man peered back at her. An amazed look came over his face. "Monica? Well, I'll be..." He gestured for his companions to lower their weapons, then stepped out from behind the Mitsubishi with a big grin. "Heck, sure is good to see you safe and sound."

"You too, Bert."

The man glanced at Jonah and Colleen briefly before returning his gaze to Monica. "Charles and the kids...they didn't make it, did they?"

Monica shook her head. "These are my friends, Jonah and Colleen. We met in Richmond." She paused briefly. "Bert, where is everybody?"

"Everyone's up at the lake. We've taken over the YMCA center. There's thirty-seven of us in total."

By now, Jonah and Colleen had joined Monica. "Any room for a couple of friendly strangers?" Jonah asked, deciding it was time to stick his oar in. "Monica told me there's good fishing at the lake."

"That'll depend on Sheriff Rollins," Bert replied curtly. "Monica was born and bred in Benton."

"Bert, these two risked their lives for me back in Richmond," Monica cut in. "I wouldn't be here if it wasn't for them. By the way, who is Sheriff Rollins? I don't think I know him. I remember Sheriff Dudley. I take it…"

Bert shook his head. "Karl didn't make it. John Rollins is the new sheriff now. Don't worry, he's a good man."

"So he's the geezer we need to butter up. Is that what you're saying?" Jonah asked.

Bert smiled briefly. "He and his four-man council make the decisions around here. Just so happens, I'm one of them." A serious look came over his face. "I've known Monica since she was twelve years old. Her father was a close friend of mine. The fact you two risked your lives for her means a lot to me. I'll be sure to put in a good word for you."

"Thank you, Bert," Colleen said quietly.

"Not at all, ma'am. Truth be told, there's plenty of room at the camp, we still got a few empty cabins. Most people have chosen to lodge in the dorms together. For company and the like, seeing as they don't have families anymore." Bert hooked a thumb back at his pickup. "Me and my men have a few supplies to get, then we'll be heading back. Why don't you guys follow behind me and I'll take you there."

Jonah rubbed his hands together enthusiastically. "Magic! I can't wait to check out this lake of yours. Monica tells me it's hopping with catfish. Soon as we get there, I'm going to go out and catch one, just in case the sheriff decides to boot us out after all."

CHAPTER 4

Rollins steered his Dodge Charger in through the Wasson Lodge entranceway, tooting his horn at his two men manning the South Cookson checkpoint ten yards past the turn. Given the uncertain circumstances, it was more important than ever that they guarded the road.

The previous afternoon, he'd received news that five trucks had left the lodge. *"They're all towing trailers, Sheriff. Looks like they're leaving for good,"* a man named Jake Calley had radioed in. *"The black guy, Walter, he's with them too."*

Rollins hadn't liked the sound of that. Walter had been due to start work on Camp Benton's micro-hydro project soon, something Rollins was anxious to get started on. Part of his reason for the visit today was to find out where Walter had gotten to.

At the top of the driveway, he pulled up outside the lodge and got out of the car. A partially-built fence surrounded the building, and at one end several bales of razor wire lay on the ground. Close by, a man sat on a pile of sandbags, his rifle next to him. As he climbed the porch steps, Rollins waved to him. The man raised his arm listlessly in return.

He stepped inside the doorway. "Chris?" he called.

A moment later, Chris poked his head out the living room door and ushered him forward. Rollins walked down the hall and entered the room to find Chris there on his own.

"Howdy," Rollins greeted him, noting his pale, tense face. The Camp Knox leader didn't exude the same abundant energy he'd witnessed the last time he's seen him. It appeared that Walter's exit had had a bad effect on camp morale.

Sitting down in an armchair opposite Chris, he got straight to the point. "My men tell me Walter and some of the others left the camp yesterday. That true?"

The expression on Chris's face soured. "He and a few others were causing trouble here," he replied. "I had to get rid of them."

Rollins frowned. "Five trucks left. That's a lot of people."

"Two belonged to some strangers that arrived yesterday. They turned out to be a rough lot, so I got rid of them as well."

Rollins had heard all about them. The checkpoint guards were instructed to report on all activity in and out of the area. It appeared the newcomers had chosen to leave with Walter too. Things had gone downhill rapidly at the lodge.

"You know where they went to?" he asked.

"No idea," Chris replied sullenly. "Sheriff, I got things to do. What exactly is it you want?"

Rollins stared at him evenly. "I'm here to assess the situation. Your security situation affects everybody. How many people are left here now?"

"Six. Soon as we complete the perimeter fence, I'll start recruiting. Don't worry, I'll have the numbers up again soon. There's plenty of people out there looking for a safe place to live." He smiled bitterly at Rollins. "Seeing as Walter has left, looks like you're going to have to find someone else for your engineering project."

Rollins shrugged. "Looks that way." He stood. There didn't seem much point in staying any longer. Chris was making that very clear. "All right, thanks for the update. Don't worry, I'll see myself out."

Back in his Charger, Rollins headed down the driveway, wondering where the hell Walter had gotten to. He hoped he was still in the area, in which case Rollins was confident the ex-Army engineer would get in touch with him. Walter didn't seem the type to welch on a deal.

***

He returned to camp to find Bert Olvan and three strangers in the staff lounge. A man and woman in their early thirties stood by the window, while Olvan sat at the table with another woman. She was a little older, perhaps in her forties.

Olvan stood up as Rollins stepped into the room and closed the door behind him.

"Uh, John, we got visitors," he said, looking a little uncomfortable.

"So I see. What's going on, Bert?"

"I found them in Benton this morning." Olvan pointed to the seated woman. "This is Monica Jeffreys."

Rollins nodded briefly at her. "Morning ma'am."

"And this is Jonah and Colleen Murphy. They're from Ireland."

Rollins raised an eyebrow. "You two are a long way from home," he said as the Irishman strode over to him, hand outstretched. He was a big-shouldered fellow with auburn hair and a broad, freckled face.

Rollins glanced down at his meaty forearms as he shook his hand. On both were several cheap-looking tattoos. One was a brightly colored ship's anchor, with a name underneath it he couldn't make out, that of his wife or mother, he was sure. On the other arm a scowling black cat stood on the number thirteen, its back stiffly arched.

"Pleased to meet yeh, Sheriff," Jonah said in a thick Irish brogue. "Yep, we're a long way from home with no way of getting back either. Me and the missus were on holidays in Orlando when this shit went—"

"When the pandemic struck," his wife cut in, shaking Rollins's hand next. Petite, pretty, with shoulder-length blonde hair, she stared at him through a set of steady blue eyes. "It's been a nightmare, but we're dealing with it."

"Glad to hear it."

"John, in case you're wondering, Monica here was born and raised in Benton," Olvan explained. "Her father, Pat Jeffreys was a good friend of mine. I don't think you knew him, he died ten years ago. Anyways, Monica has been living in Savannah this past while. She drove up this morning. I found her on Station Road, trying to figure out where in heck's name everyone was."

Rollins smiled. "Lucky she bumped into you. It might have taken a while to figure out where we'd all gotten to."

"I know this area well, Sheriff," Monica replied. "After checking the farms, the lake was next on my list. I used to bring my husband and children here every summer. After my mother died, I held onto the house on Wilson Street to keep our connection with the place. Charles and the kids loved coming here…" Her voice trailed off. "Of course, everything is different now. I'm the only one in the family to survive."

"I take it you met these two in Savannah?" Rollins asked, glancing over at the Irish couple.

"Yes, I met them yesterday. They helped me out of a tight spot…a…a nasty situation."

"It's true," Olvan cut in. "This fine couple risked their lives for Monica. Drove all guns blazing into a supermarket parking lot to save her from a gang of men who had nothing but bad intentions toward her. That right, Jonah?"

"A bunch of skangers had it in for her, no question about it," Jonah replied, nodding his head vigorously. "We bate them off quick enough though. I did the driving—Jason Statham style—while Colleen popped away at them with her

Armalite. Can't deny we had a couple of hairy moments, but it turned out all right in the end."

The more Jonah talked, speaking faster and faster with his thick accent, the more trouble Rollins had understanding him. He nodded politely. "Sounds like you did a fine job." He stared at the couple. "What are your plans now?"

Jonah flashed a high-beam smile at him. "Funny yeh should mention that. Before we met Monica, we weren't exactly sure where we were heading. Seeing as we're here now, we were hoping we might stay a while." He glanced at Olvan. "Bertie tells me you're the head honcho around these parts, and we need to run it past you. What do you say, Sheriff?"

Rollins hesitated. Everyone at the camp was from Benton. So far they hadn't allowed any strangers in. While friendly, and obviously strong and able, there was something about the Irishman's restless eyes and unbridled energy he found slightly disconcerting. He needed to be careful.

Jonah caught his look. "Ah, don't be giving yerself a hernia over it, Sheriff. Not a bother," he said, smiling ruefully. "Give us a jiffy and me and the missus will be out of yer hair quicker than a toupee in a hurricane. Yeh get them around these parts, don't yis?"

"John…they did save Monica's life," Olvan said quietly. "That counts for a lot in my book."

"In my book too, Bert." Rollins made his decision. "I'll run it past the council to make it official, but you can take it from me and Bert, the two of you can stay."

Jonah grinned. "Ah, yeh had me going there for a minute, Sheriff. Thought you were going to give us the right old boot. Yeh won't regret it. I'm pretty handy on carpentry and the likes. Anything you need done around here, just give me a shout."

"Thank you. Will do."

Jonah continued. "Yeh wouldn't have an old paddleboat lying around somewhere, would yeh? Seeing as it's such a gorgeous day, I wouldn't mind getting out on the lake and doing a bit of fishing. I'm told the catfish are practically leppin' out of the water. That's so, Bertie?"

Olvan glanced over at Rollins, grinning. "That's right, Jonah. Catfish, bass, crappie, bluegill. We got them all here."

"Magic!" Jonah exclaimed, rubbing his hands gleefully. "Finally, I get to do a bit of fishing!"

Unable to help himself, Rollins broke out into a smile too. The excitable Irishman's humor was infectious, even if he could barely understand a word he said.

"Don't worry," he told him. "We'll see to it you get out on the lake. It's the very least we can do for bringing one of our own home safe and sound."

CHAPTER 5

The eight members of the newly-formed "Jack's River Camp" group sat in a circle under the shade of a large oak tree on the east side of the Alaculsy Valley. Nearby, the sound of rushing waters could be heard as they tumbled down a bouldered riverbed.

The group was conducting its first official meeting.

"First things first," Walter began. Leaning against the base of the tree, he sat cross-legged, holding a small notebook in his hand. "You've all had a chance to take a look around. What do y'all make of our new home?"

That morning, Cody and Emma had risen early to explore the surrounding area, and hiked deeper into Georgia along a tributary of the Conasauga. Following a well-worn trail, they'd passed through valleys profuse with wildflowers and blooming mountain laurel, and traversed lush green forests rich with moss, fern, and rhododendron.

"If this isn't paradise, where on Earth is?" Emma had asked as the two bathed in a deep pool. Above them, cool mountain waters tumbled over a rocky outcrop and onto their heads. After making love, they'd headed back to camp, just in time for the group's first meeting.

"It's beautiful here," Emma said, in reply to Walter's question. "So peaceful."

Walter smiled. "Let's do everything we can to keep it that way." He paused briefly. "Now, some of you have requested that I should accept the role as leader of this group. Unlike a certain someone we all know, I think everyone should be given a chance to put their names forward for the position. So, if anyone wants to, now would be the time to do that."

Everyone looked around the circle at each other, shaking their heads. Ralph was the first to speak. "From what I've heard, you got the smarts around here. Go for it."

"Absolutely," Greta said, sitting opposite him. "It's unanimous, Walter. It's you."

Walter nodded his head graciously. "Thank you. I'd be honored to take the role. And you can all rest easy in knowing that I'm not the power-hungry type. Anytime the group decides there's someone better served to do the job, I'll be happy to step down."

Sitting to his right, Pete chuckled. "They say power is a drug, Walter. Who knows how you'll feel when the time actually comes."

"Pete, I told you not to give the game away," Walter replied, winking at him. "All right. When the group gets bigger, we can think about appointing a council. For now, we can decide things among the eight of us, everyone agreed?"

Around the circle, everybody nodded in assent.

"Good. Today, let's stick to our immediate needs. Things like security arrangements and scavenging runs. Recruitment is also going to be real important. I don't think a *build it and they will come* policy is going to work these days. First though, I thought we'd start off with a fun item. 'Jack's River Camp'? Don't know about the rest of you, but that sounds kinda lame to me. Can anyone think of a better name, something with a little more *oomph*?" His eyes rested on Cody. "I say we give you first shot at it. Any ideas, kid?"

Cody thought for a moment. "Yeah," he said hesitantly. "If it's okay with everyone, I'd like to name it 'Camp Eastwood'. In memory of my father's favorite actor."

A murmur of assent went around the circle. Walter nodded approvingly.

"Very fitting. Camp Eastwood it is. All right, let's talk about recruitment. We got the ideal location to build a great community, we're just short a few people, that's all. There's gangs fifteen, twenty strong, roaming the area. Sooner or later, they're going to find their way here. With only eight of us, it'll be a tall order to defend this place, so we need to move on this fast. Anyone here like to volunteer to go out on a recruitment tour and bring back a bunch of able-bodied men and women?"

Pete shot up his hand. "I'll go. I think I can find the right people." He smiled weakly. "I made an error in judgment once before. I won't make that same mistake again."

Walter nodded. "Agreed. Hard won lessons are always the best ones. You'll need a couple more people to go with you, though. It's too dangerous out there for just one man." He looked around the group. "Who else wants to volunteer to go with Pete? Somebody good with a gun."

Cody glanced at Emma, a questioning look in his eye. She gave him a quick nod of her head. He was about to reply when Ralph spoke up. "If you need someone good with a gun, I'm your man."

"I can vouch for that. He's *real* good," Maya said. "I'll come too. In a situation like this, having a woman with you can only help with the recruiting."

"Thanks guys," Pete replied with a pleased grin. "I couldn't wish for two better traveling companions."

"That's the perfect recruitment team," Walter agreed, a satisfied look on his face. "All right, the day after tomorrow, you need to do a sweep of the nearby towns. First time around, don't bring back more than three or four people. We need to assimilate folk into the group carefully. That's one thing Chris was right about."

"True," Ralph said. "Even one bad dude is a problem." He shrugged. "Not that it'll be my decision. I'm just the muscle."

Pete grinned. "Between me and Maya, I'm sure we'll figure it out. You can all look forward to seeing some friendly new faces here soon."

Walter next went onto security arrangements. Cody glanced over at Emma and smiled. These were good, strong people, and he felt confident about how everything was going. No doubt challenges still awaited them, but with Walter at the helm, he felt their chances of survival were good. Time would tell.

CHAPTER 6

"*Jaysus,* that was some journey, wasn't it, love? Wouldn't want to do that again in a hurry."

Beer in hand, Jonah leaned against the porch rail of Chickasaw, the cabin Bert Olvan had just assigned the couple ten minutes ago. Twenty feet away, Lake Ocoee's azure waters sparkled invitingly in the sun.

He sighed contentedly. "Finally, we can relax. "

Inside, Colleen lay on the bed, resting. Their new dwelling slept up to six people, but the couple had the place to themselves for now. With eighteen cabins in total at the camp, there had been no need for them to share.

The cabin was cozy. It had its own bathroom, and a small kitchen with a gas oven and stovetop. Without running water, they would have to fill a bucket from the lake to flush the toilet, Olvan had explained earlier.

"That's no bother, Bertie," Jonah had replied cheerfully. "Been in a lot worse places than this on me travels. Yeh wouldn't believe the state of the campsite I stayed in Wexford last summer. The jakes was a real kip. I tell yeh, the smell was bleedin' brutal."

"That's enough, Jonah," Colleen said firmly. "I'm sure Bert doesn't want to hear about your camping

27

experiences in Ireland right now. We've got more important things to think about."

Olvan chuckled. "Tonight over a beer, I'd like to hear all about it. You look like someone who's got a few stories to tell."

Jonah grinned. "Sound man, Bertie. Yeh might even catch me singing a song or two while I'm at it."

With that, Olvan had clapped Jonah on the shoulder and left, strolling over to the nearby, and appropriately named, Three Sisters cabin, where Monica was sharing living quarters with two women around the same age as herself.

Finishing off his beer, Jonah poked his head in through the door and stared over at Colleen. "Right, love. I'll go and fetch the rest of the gear from the car. After that, I'm going to grab a rod and take a proper gander at this lake. Bertie says he'll have a boat ready for me. Yeh fancy coming?"

"I got a headache," Colleen said, lying on the bed. "I just want to relax for now. When you get back, I'll prepare some lunch. We'll have our last meal together before I take our provisions over to the dining hall."

The one stipulation Sheriff Rollins had made on allowing the couple to join the Benton group was that they agreed to hand over their foodstuffs to be shared communally. Neither of them had objected. They were joining a large, well-organized group, and it made sense that something as critical as food was shared among everyone.

Before showing them to their cabins, Olvan had introduced the three to Mary Sadowski who, as well as being the firearms instructor at the camp, held the keys to kitchen storeroom.

Jonah had stared at the spry sixty-year-old lady, grinning. "You're perfect for the job, Mary, there's not a pick on yeh. Doesn't look like yer scoffing down the Jammie Dodgers when nobody's looking."

The Irishman had received a frosty stare in reply, before Sadowski had gone on to explain that meals were cooked three times a day and eaten over at the dining hall. There was oatmeal and instant coffee for breakfast, pasta and soup for lunch, and freshly grilled meat or fish in the evenings, supplied by the hunters who went out in search of game each day.

Jonah was thankful she hadn't mention anything about alcohol. He needed that in easy reach, not under the stern eye of somebody like Mary Sadowski. He had a funny feeling they might not see eye to eye on what Jonah considered a *normal* daily allowance.

"Grand," he said, smiling at Colleen. "Crack open one of them tins of spaghetti and meatballs and we'll tuck into it soon as I get back. Then I'll take everything over to Mary. The auld battleax can put it under lock and key." He winked at Colleen. "Maybe we'll keep a packet of biscuits here on the sly. Whaddeyeh say?"

"Jonah. No."

"Ah, go on, love. It's not like—"

"Jonah, I said no!"

Jonah put on a glum face. "Colleen, you're so...so..."

"By the book?"

Jonah grinned. "That's it. Something tells me you and Mary are going to get on like a house on fire."

With that, he closed the door behind him and strode over to where the Nissan was parked in the lot. The sooner he finished unpacking, the sooner he'd get to go fishing. Somewhere in that lake was a twenty pound catfish with his name written all over it. He was going to haul it in and give it a great big kiss. Right on the smacker!

CHAPTER 7

In Charlotte, North Carolina, Simone Holmes rode down the middle of the LYNX Blue Line railroad track, keeping the engine of her Yamaha 125cc motorcycle at a low rev. Heading south, the next station was Archdale, not that she intended going that far. Her destination was the Aldi supermarket on the Old Pineville Road, a mile short of the station.

Simone hadn't eaten in over twenty-four hours. Not only was food scarce these days, it was dangerous to come by, too. What remained in the supermarkets was controlled by the newly-formed gangs that had sprung up over the city this past week with alarming speed. They'd taken over all sorts of places, and many gas stations and drugstores were under their control too. But food mattered the most. If you controlled the food, you controlled the people, and a person who hadn't eaten in days was easy to press into the ranks in exchange for some meager rations.

There were several reasons why Simone had no intentions of joining a gang. The main one being that her father, Clarence Holmes, a black officer and 25-year veteran of the Charlotte-Mecklenburg Police Department, wouldn't have approved. Although he'd died eight days ago, it just didn't sit right with her. Her father had instilled in her a strong sense of morals. She had no intention of letting them go that quickly.

Soon after driving across the Tyvola Road overpass, she pulled up to a stop. On her left, obscured by a dense line of evergreens bordering the track, was the supermarket.

She cut the engine and dismounted the Yamaha, wheeling it around so that it faced in the direction she'd come. Her original plan had been to hide it behind the tree line, but at the last minute she'd decided against it. If she had to leave in a hurry, better that her machine faced in the right direction, ready to go. Besides, no one ever passed along the railroad tracks these days, as far as she could tell.

With her rucksack on her back, she crossed the tracks and walked through the dense but narrow band of trees. Emerging out the other side, she crouched behind one of them. Not more than thirty yards away was the back entrance to the Aldi, a large one-story building about two hundred feet long.

The huge steel doors of the delivery gates were closed, and she knew that the front was heavily guarded. Earlier that day, she'd passed by and seen several armed men lounging by their vehicles, drinking beer and passing a joint around. That was fine with Simone. She had a more devious plan to break into the supermarket.

Crouching low, she made the thirty yard sprint over to the southwest corner of the building. Sticking close to the wall, she darted across to a stack of pallets stored fifteen feet high. Next to them, a refrigerated trailer stood parked. Its doors had been busted open and there was nothing inside.

By sticking her toes between the gaps in the pallets, she climbed nimbly up them and, once on top, clambered up onto the trailer. From there, the supermarket's asphalt roof was in easy reach, and she hauled herself up onto it.

She treaded softly over to a large air conditioning vent, where she took out a screwdriver from her jacket pocket and began removing the screws from the front panel. As soon as they were all out, she lifted the panel off and placed it gently on the ground, then climbed into the metal housing to where a set of enormous louvers faced down onto the supermarket floor thirty feet below.

She took the rucksack off her back, pulled out a length of rope, and fixed it onto a thick steel pipe that ran along the wall. Then she poked her head out through the louver's plastic shutters and took a look around.

Other than for the faint glow of daylight coming from the front entrance, it was dark inside the building. Once she was sure there was no one around, she dropped the rope to the ground, then squeezed her body through the louvers. Grabbing the rope, she shimmied down it, using the knots she'd tied on it at evenly-spaced intervals for grip.

When she hit the floor, she pulled out a flashlight from her pocket and switched it on. Shrugging the rucksack from her shoulders, she crept up and down the aisles, loading it with foodstuffs. In went cans of tuna, beef, ham, and turkey meat, then at the dry foods section, packs of spicy ramen noodles—her favorite.

Reaching one of the outer loops, her eyes lit up when she came across a cookie tower. Careful not to make any noise, she crammed her pack with peanut butter, oatmeal, and shortbread cookies, along with crackers, pretzels, and granola bars.

She scoured the aisles to find where the bottled water was stored. After a long search, with only the tiny flashlight to guide her, she finally found it on the far side of the store.

She had just put three 1.5 liter bottles inside her pack when she heard the sound of voices. Heart racing, she instantly turned off her flashlight.

By the entrance, a powerful torch switched on. There was the sound of footsteps, then the low drawl of a man's voice spoke out.

"Hot damn, Ledell. Drinking beer and eating pretzels all day. Now that's what I call a dream job. What say you, buddy?"

"Fuck yeah," a second voice replied, even gruffer than the first. "We need to milk this for all its worth. Tomorrow it's back to guarding some shithole part of town again."

The first man chuckled. "I hear you, bro. Time to hit the beer section again."

Simone hadn't come across the beer section. She just hoped it wasn't anywhere near her. Crouched down on the floor, she quietly zipped up her rucksack and slung it up onto her shoulders.

As she rose to her feet, the flashlight moved away in the opposite direction. She let out a sigh of relief. It looked like the beer section was in a different part of the store. Hopefully the men would just grab their beers and head back outside again.

Something else dawned on her. A fear that was realized moments later.

"Shit, Rico," Ledell called out. "What's that hanging from the ceiling? Holy fuck!"

Simone froze as a torch angled its beam toward the ceiling, to where her rope dangled out of the air con unit. Her one and only means of escape from the building was now gone.

She thought hard. If she was quick, perhaps she could sneak past the guards at the front entrance. With a little luck, she could bolt around the side of the building and get back to the tree line without getting shot.

That option was taken away from her a moment later.

"Louie, Hector…we got an intruder in here! Get your asses over to the doorway!" one of the men yelled.

There was a crackle of static, then a voice responded over a radio. *"Okay, Ledell. On our way now."*

Simone's next instinct was to look for somewhere to hole up and just hope that the men presumed she'd already left the building. It was a good idea. The only trouble was, there didn't seem anywhere good to hide.

Scurrying along the row, she headed toward the side wall farthest away from the men. When she reached it, she saw that in the corner, thirty feet away, was what looked like a staffroom door. If it was unlocked, perhaps there was somewhere inside she could hide.

In a low crouch, she headed for it, checking each horizontal aisle as she passed by to make sure neither of the men stood along it.

She made it three rows from the end when a voice called out behind her. "Stop right there, you sonofabitch!"

She spun around to see a muscular black man in a sleeveless tank top standing at the corner of one of the aisles, pointing a pistol at her. He wore a baseball cap turned at an angle, and a heavy gold rope chain dangled from his neck. "Over here, Rico!" he shouted over his shoulder. "I've found him."

The man stepped forward warily, keeping his flashlight trained on Simone. When he got closer, his shoulders dropped and he lowered his weapon. "Hey, it's only a girl! She can't be more than sixteen years old either."

There was the sound of footsteps, and another man appeared a couple of aisles behind him, a light-skinned Hispanic wearing a white T-shirt, baggy pants, and a bandana tied around his forehead.

He looked Simone up and down appreciatively as he drew alongside his companion. "Why, Ledell, she's a fine little thing too. Look at her, half grown up and nearly all woman. Sweetheart, how old are you?"

"F-Fifteen," Simone replied nervously, blinking in the harsh glare of the flashlight.

A broad grin came over the man's face. "Bro, you thinking what I'm thinking?"

"Hell yeah," Ledell growled. "Must be our lucky day. We got booze, we got weed. Now we get to have a little fun too."

"Please, mister. D-don't..." Simone stammered, thrusting both hands inside her jacket pockets nervously.

"Don't what, little girl?"

Both men stepped forward, their intentions written all over their faces.

Simone backed away. "Don't make me do this."

Rico sniggered. "You got any idea what she's talking about?"

"Nope, cos it don't matter a damn," Ledell replied with a throaty drawl. "Only thing that matters right now is how fine this girl is." He took another step forward. "Come here, sweetheart. Come to Daddy."

There was another chuckle from Rico.

"All right…." Simone raised her right hand still inside her jacket pocket and extended it forward. Clutched tightly in her grip was her father's compact Glock 43, his backup weapon. At the range, he'd taught her how to shoot well with it too. "Seeing as you're the biggest asshole."

"What the f—" Ledell stopped in his tracks, staring at her in disbelief. Desperately, he raised his pistol, which he'd held loosely by his side, gangster style. Before he could take aim, Simone fired twice in quick succession, and two nine millimeter rounds tore into his chest and stomach. With a grunt, he staggered back, clutching his belly with one hand.

Simone swiveled the Glock and pointed it at Rico next. Another two rounds ripped into his chest. With a low moan, he slumped to the ground.

There was no time to hang around. Simone darted down the aisle closest to her and raced toward the center of the supermarket. From the building entrance, she heard voices shouting, then the sound of running footsteps.

Reaching the center aisle, she sprinted over to the rope and scrambled up it. The weight of her pack made the going tough, and she was thankful for having taken the time to make the knots in the rope, helping to give her better purchase.

She reached the ceiling, breathing hard. With her pack on, getting back inside the aircon unit was a lot harder than before, and she had to push down hard on the louver shutters, breaking them open before clambering inside. Below, several flashlights were now combing the building. She quickly pulled up the rope so that the men would have no idea of her location, then climbed up through the metal casing and back out onto the roof. Temporarily blinded by the sunlight, she stumbled forward, then ran toward the corner of the building.

When she reached it, she peered cautiously over the edge to see a red pickup parked at the back entrance. Two men stood by the delivery gate, no doubt trying to figure out how an intruder had gotten inside. With a sense of relief, she saw that there was no one along the south wall where the pallets were stacked.

Barely pausing, she slid her body over the side of the wall and jumped down onto the trailer roof, then climbed down the stack of pallets again. As soon as her feet hit the concrete, she sprinted toward the tree line, praying that the guards around the corner didn't choose that moment to continue their sweep of the building.

She reached the trees and ran straight through them, pine needles scraping her face and arms as she rushed past. At one point, her feet tangled in the undergrowth and she fell to the ground. Scrambling to her feet again, she pushed through the last of the branches and, with a sigh of relief, spotted her Yamaha parked ten yards away.

She ran over and jumped on, then slotted the key in the ignition. As the engine came to life, she looked behind her but saw no sign of any activity. Letting out the clutch, she raced up the track, not slowing until she was well past the far side of the Tyvola Road overpass. Finally, she could relax.

It was time to go home for her last evening in the city. Things were getting too dangerous here. Tomorrow, at first light, she would leave. She was done with this town.

CHAPTER 8

The following morning at dawn, a convoy of two pickup trucks and a motorcycle set off from Old Fort. Turning onto the Old Federal Road, they drove north for eight miles until they reached Sloans Gap Road, then headed east.

Leading the way, Russ Willis rode his Suzuki VStrom. Mason Bonner followed next, sitting behind the wheel of his black GMC Canyon, his bodyguard Doney beside him. At their security firm in Knoxville, Mason had been a driver, and he still liked to drive. Behind him, two crew members occupied the back seats, while in the truck bed, a further two sat with their rifles sticking out over the sides. The second pickup was similarly configured.

The formation passed through a section of thick pine forest. Coming around a tight bend, the VStrom's brake lights came on. Mason slowed down when Russ stuck his right hand out.

Moments later, the motorbike turned up a narrow lane, signposted Casson Road. Almost immediately, the lane cut hard to the right. Turning the corner, Russ drove another twenty yards and pulled over to the side of the road.

Mason came to a stop beside him. He opened his door and jumped out as the trailing vehicle drew up behind him. "We're too far from the damned road," he said irritatedly as Russ strolled up to him. "What the hell we doing here?"

"Relax, Mason. This is the hideout spot while we wait for somebody to come by this way. It could be a few hours." Russ pointed back toward the Sloans Gap Road. "Give me three of your men and I'll go set the trap. Won't take more than twenty minutes. Once it's ready, I'll ride up to the YMCA camp. Soon as someone leaves, I'll radio ahead so you can get ready."

Mason breathed a little easier. "All right, that'll work." He ordered the two men sitting in the Canyon's load bed to get out.

After the second man jumped down off the tailgate, Russ pointed back into the truck. "Grab that chainsaw," he told him. "We're going to need it."

With a grunt, the crew member leaned over and dragged out the gas-powered Kawasaki chainsaw Russ had stored there earlier.

When the man made to hand it over to him, Russ said, "No, you carry it. It's you that going to be using it."

Without another word, he set off down the lane in the direction of the junction. The two crew members exchanged surly glances, then followed after him.

Mason chuckled. Russ's cunning and intelligence was serving him well, but the devious runt wasn't making any new friends, that was for sure.

CHAPTER 9

Cody sat by himself on his trailer steps sipping coffee. A few minutes ago, Emma had gone off to Walter's trailer where Greta was in the process of setting up a makeshift clinic. She needed help sorting out the medical supplies that she'd hastily grabbed at the lodge the previous day, and Emma had offered to help her.

Cody had been busy too. That morning, he'd been part of an armed detail that had ridden out of camp to source badly needed supplies. Riding in two pickups they'd taken the old Highway 2 and cut west across the Cohutta, emerging onto Route 411 at a town called Chatsworth. Driving through the empty streets, they'd ventured fifteen miles farther to reach Dalton City. Being a relatively unknown town, they hoped they might have some luck in getting everything they needed. By now, Chattanooga and Cleveland had been pretty much stripped clean.

Their luck was in. On an out of the way street, they came across a builder supplier whose entrance gate was still intact. Breaking into the yard, they filled the trucks with carpentry tools, screws, nails, timber, barbed wire, and a host of other things Walter had listed down for them.

Before returning to camp, they stopped at a Walmart and managed to find the exact same radio handsets that

Walter had brought with him from Knoxville. They also grabbed a chainsaw, gardening gloves, and a stack of four-foot plastic flower-box planters. Cody had no idea what Walter wanted them for. To grow vegetables, he presumed. With both trucks stocked to the brim, they'd made an uneventful journey home.

He checked his watch. In a few minutes, the group was due to start work on building the camp's defenses. Walter was anxious to start right away and utilize Pete, Ralph, and Maya before they left in the morning. The camp would be considerably more exposed while they were gone. He drained his coffee and stood up. Time to get back to work.

On arrival the previous day, the group had driven their vehicles off the highway and up an unpaved road where, at the top of a small rise, they unhitched the trailers. Nestled between two hills, the road was out of sight from anyone passing through the Alaculsy Valley.

Standing next to his pickup, Walter stood waiting for everyone. "All right people. First thing I'd like to do is go through a few security principles," he said when all seven had arrived and stood around him in a semicircle. "I need you to have a clear understanding on how I want our defenses set up."

He pointed down the hill in the direction of the highway. "Up here on this saddle offers us a sloping field of fire against anybody coming up from the valley." He pointed along the dirt road in the other direction, where it cut deeper into the hills. "This route behind us gives us a means of escape if we need it. That's important. The ability to retreat from an overwhelming force is one of the key requirements of a good defensive position.

"As discussed, as soon as we have a larger group, we'll move down to the farm, but while Pete and the others are away, vigilance and concealment are our two best defense strategies. That makes this a good spot for now."

Down in the valley and out of sight from the camp was what had been a cattle farm with several outbuildings.

There was no sign of the cattle. Where they had gone was anyone's guess. However, the land was flat, and the Conasauga River flowed along the eastern border of the property. While it was a prime location, in Walter's view, it was too exposed a place to defend with such a small group.

"What are you saying, Walter?" Greta asked, her brow furrowing. "You intend on us just hunkering down here, or are we actually going to set up some type of defenses?"

Walter smiled. "Of course we are. We're going to build an easy to make, yet effective, defensive position. That's why I sent some of you out to Dalton City earlier." He pointed over to the bales of barbed wire they'd brought back. They were stacked by one of the trailers, alongside the rest of the supplies. "Ideally, I would have preferred coiled razor wire, but it's hard to find. Other than for US military properties, it was against most building codes to use it. These rolls of farm barbed wire will do fine, though."

He walked over to the Tundra and pulled out his notebook through the open window. Placing it on the hood, he indicated for everyone to gather around him.

On the pad, he'd sketched out the camp's terrain, marking out various positions such as where they should park their trucks and trailers, where and how the barbed wire should be lain to construct what he called "low wire entanglements". Also, where the trees they would cut down with the chainsaw should be placed at the bottom of the hill, preventing easy access into the camp.

Lastly, he pointed over to the planter boxes. "Pack those to the brim with dirt," he instructed. Turning back to the map, he indicated the exact positions where they should be deployed. "These will stop any vehicle that tries to storm the camp."

"How many people will these defenses hold back?" Emma asked. "You told us some of the gangs number fifteen, twenty people."

"Depends on a lot of things," Walter replied. "How well-armed they are, how resolute *we* are. Typically, though, defenders gain around a three to one advantage. Positioned up here in the hills, I'd say that's about right." He pointed to the higher of the two hills. "See up there? From the top, it commands a view of both approaches into the valley. We're going to place someone up there day and night to keep watch. Remember what I said: concealment is our first priority. If they don't see us, most people coming this way will probably just pass on through."

"What if they decide to occupy the farm?" Ralph asked.

"The farm is ours," Walter replied firmly. "For now, we got a better chance of holding it from here than being overrun down in the valley."

Greta stared at him. "So when do we start keeping lookout?"

"Right now. And you've got first watch." Walter pulled his binoculars from off his neck and handed them to her. "Before you leave, I'll key in our new radios. You can take one up with you."

Greta nodded obediently. Cody couldn't help but smile to see her pacified by Walter's gentle but firm demeanor. Greta was quite a handful, and had naturally slipped into position as second in command at the camp.

"How about nighttime?" he asked. "It's going to be harder to keep watch. Guess we'll just have to look out for car lights and the sound of engines, right?"

Walter nodded. "Exactly. I got something that will help us. Back in Knoxville, I picked up a pair of night vision glasses. Even if they come on foot, we'll be able to spot anyone long before they see us." He grinned. "All right people, enough talk. Time for us to roll up our sleeves and break into a sweat."

***

"That Walter, he's one smart dude. Got a good attitude too," Clete said, puffing a little as he and Cody dragged a large sapling across the track a hundred yards down the hill from the camp. It marked the perimeter of cleared ground that Walter called a "kill zone," an area where any would-be intruders would be exposed as they approached their position. Earlier, Walter had split the group into pairs, and Clete and Cody had been chosen to work together. They had just cut down the tree, tied it to the back of Clete's pickup, and hauled it down the hill.

"He sure does." Cody stood up and rubbed his hands together, removing the dirt from them. "We're going to build something good here. A place that's got a real future."

"Can't argue with that." Clete paused a moment. "Hey kid, what say you and me go into the forest tomorrow morning? See if we can't get some fresh game for everyone."

Cody's eyes lit up. "That'd be cool. With everything that's been going on, I haven't had a chance to go hunting lately."

"I was thinking of something a little different," Clete said. "You ever trap before?"

"Nope, but I'd sure like to learn," Cody said eagerly. Trapping was an essential survival skill in a place like the Cohutta, and he was anxious to learn everything he could from the man they called Mr. Hillbilly.

Clete grinned. "It's the lazy man's way of getting meat. Once you've set your traps, you can spend the rest of the day getting drunk. Next time you swing by, you got a meal waiting for you. Get to sleep early. Don't let that pretty girl of yours keep you up all night. Tomorrow at dawn, I'll be over to pick you up."

CHAPTER 10

At 10:30 a.m., Ned Granger collected a team of three men and headed out of Camp Benton in his Nissan Titan. His destination was Cleveland, in search of more supplies so that he could complete work on the final stage of the camp's defenses.

Granger had recently constructed a secondary defense line he called the Ring, a fallback position centered around the main square in the event that the camp got overrun in an attack. On the south side of the Ring, he planned on creating an emergency extraction route down to South Beach, from where the group could escape by boat across the Baker Creek inlet.

While he sincerely hoped this was a scenario that would never materialize, they had to be prepared for all eventualities. With the camp located on a peninsula and surrounded on three sides by water, it was important that their escape route was carefully planned.

Sitting beside him in the front passenger seat was Marcus Welby, a young man in his twenties whose father Granger had known before the epidemic. Behind in the truck bed were Bob Harper and Joe Macey, two men he had barely known before the disaster. In their thirties, both were hard workers, tough, and determined. They were good with weapons too. Just the kind of people needed at the camp.

As a man who'd seen plenty of combat during the first Gulf War, Granger had figured out pretty quickly which of the men would be any use to him in the heat of battle. He estimated that, out of the seventeen adult men, perhaps eight or nine would show true grit in a firefight. As for the fifteen women, other than for Mary Sadowski, it was hard for him to judge. Granger had never fought alongside women before. At some stage, perhaps sooner rather than later, he knew that might change.

His mind wandered back to the previous evening when Rollins had introduced him to the three new arrivals. Learning their story and briefly studying their demeanors, he reckoned they could be relied on in a tight situation, particularly the Irish couple. Colleen, the petite blonde woman, had a steely look in her eye. As for her husband, though barely intelligible with his thick Dublin brogue, he had the look of someone who had been around the block before, probably several times.

"Ned, where are we going to get supplies?" Marcus asked, breaking him away from his thoughts. "They're getting hard to find now. At the Home Depot in Chat yesterday, just about everything worth taking was gone."

"Don't worry, Bert's given me some places to check out," Granger told him. "After thirty years in construction, he's gotten to know just about every hardware store and builder's yard in the area."

"That's good. Hopefully we'll find everything we need."

They reached Sloans Gap Road. Granger steered the Nissan around a sharp bend. To either side of the road, dense pine forest grew almost all the way up to the asphalt. Straightening out the wheel, he picked up speed again.

Ahead, he spotted movement. Two men crouched on either end of a large sapling that had been dragged across the road. Both held rifles, pointing at the oncoming Nissan.

Granger jammed his foot on the brakes. "Ambush!" he yelled.

Welby immediately grabbed his rifle. He slid the selector switch off safety and poked the barrel out the window as the Nissan came to a stop a hundred yards before the tree.

About to reverse, Granger glanced in his rearview mirror. Behind him, two pickup trucks tore around the corner and screeched to a stop. In the truck bed, Harper and Meyer had seen them too. Squatting on their heels, they raised their rifles, aiming their sights toward the trucks.

Granger peered out through the windscreen, trying to gauge whether he could drive along the side of the road and squeeze past the felled sapling or not. The bandits had positioned it perfectly, though. There wasn't a hope in hell.

A fusillade of gunfire suddenly opened up from behind the tree line where several men had lain in wait. Granger barely had time to react when the front passenger window shattered. Instantly, blood sprayed across the windscreen and Welby keeled face forward onto the dashboard. Horrified, Granger saw that several rounds had caught him in head.

In the load bed, Joe Macey returned fire into the forest in short bursts. Hunkered down below the tailgate, Bob Harper started shooting at the two pickups parked on either side of the road.

There was no hope for Welby. He had died instantaneously. Granger snatched his radio from off the seat divider, then opened his door and jumped out onto the road.

Back at the bend, bandits spilled out of both vehicles, rifles in hand. Taking cover behind the tree line, they opened fire on the exposed Nissan. In the other direction, the men behind the sapling scattered into the forest, getting out of the line of fire from their own men.

Granger crouched behind his door and pulled out a Ruger P95 from his holster. He shouted up to Harper and Meyer in the truck bed. "Bob, Joe, get down here!" Currently, the driver's side of the truck provided the greatest shelter from the gunfire.

He jabbed the Talk button on his radio. "Bravo Two to base. Ambush on Sloans Gap Road!" he screamed into it. "There's at least ten of them. Repeat, ambush on Sloans Gap Road."

Bob Harper jumped over the side of the truck to join him as bullets whistled around them.

Thud, thud, thud.

Several more rounds ripped through the metal structure of the vehicle.

"Where's Joe?" Granger yelled at Harper.

Harper shook his head grimly. "He's gone."

The two men's only hope of survival was to escape into the forest. Granger pointed ahead as bullets continued to whine around their ears. "Bob, we got to move!"

Harper nodded, and in a low crouch, the two men darted across the road heading for the trees.

Granger made it five yards when he heard a short grunt, then Harper was no longer running alongside him. A moment later, a bullet tore into his foot. Stumbling forward, another caught him in the forearm and the Ruger fell from his grip. He hobbled on, waiting for a final bullet to finish him off. A round caught him in the shin, shattering the bone, and he fell to the ground in agonizing pain.

He tried to rise to his feet as the shooting petered out. "Stop, mister, you got nowhere to run!" a deep voice bellowed.

His position hopeless, Granger sat back on the ground. He faced his attackers, raising both hands in the air. Ten feet away, Bob Harper lay face down on the grass verge. Several bullets had caught him in the head, and his face was twisted into an ugly grimace. Granger knew instantly he was dead.

Staring over at the Nissan, he saw Joe Macey's body drooped over the side panel. Granger was the last man alive. He doubted he would remain so much longer.

A group of eight or so men emerged from the forest. They fanned out across the road and strode toward him.

Leading the group was a huge baldheaded man with a few wisps of long sandy hair at the back. He stopped ten feet from Granger and stood there grinning at him.

"I think it's fair to say you weren't expecting that, were you?" he said in a low-toned voice, the same that had called out earlier.

Granger spat on the ground. "Sonofabitch," he said hoarsely. "There was no need for that."

A small, weedy man in a red and black jacket with unkempt brown hair stepped forward to stand beside the giant. In one hand, he carried a motorcycle helmet.

"Now see, that's where you're wrong," he said, smirking at Granger. "And in case you're wondering, the reason you're still alive is cos I know who you are. You're the sheriff's second-in-command, ain't you? I'm sure you got plenty of interesting things to tell us."

CHAPTER 11

Simone rode north up the Billy Graham Parkway, the rays of the bright morning sun beaming down on her. Weaving through a line of abandoned cars piled up in front of the exit, she drove past Douglas International Airport on her left, picked up Interstate 85, and headed west out of the city.

She traveled light. Inside a waterproof bag strapped to the motorcycle tank were her only possessions: a spare set of clothes, and the food and water she'd stolen from the Aldi supermarket the previous day.

Slung across her back was a Mossberg Patriot Bantam, the hunting rifle her father had bought her recently. Weighing only six and a half pounds, it was designed for smaller statured shooters such as herself. Chambered in .243 Winchester, it had a light recoil, and at the shooting range she had shot well with it, though she'd yet to hunt a live animal. That would be the real test.

The previous evening, she'd ditched her Yamaha 125 and taken a red Honda 250 CRF parked in a neighbor's driveway at the top of the street. Breaking into the house hadn't been a pleasant experience. The stink of rotten bodies inside was almost unbearable. Thankfully, she soon found the Honda's key on top of the refrigerator and had rushed straight out again.

The 250cc machine was the biggest model she felt comfortable riding. Simone was only five two. Gassing it up had been easy. She'd simply bust open the fuel cap off another motorcycle, dropped a piece of hose into the tank, and siphoned the fuel out into a plastic can. She'd even managed to do it without getting a mouthful of gas.

In her jacket pocket was a road map. On it, she'd marked out a route to Gainesville, Georgia. Two hundred miles away, riding on an empty highway, she estimated she would make the trip in three hours. Plenty of time to arrive before nightfall.

Her reason for choosing Gainesville was simple. Her father was originally from the town, and her Uncle Tyler still lived there with his wife, a fourteen-year-old daughter, and a seven-year-old son. Being a small city, more of a country town, she hoped it would be safer than Charlotte.

It was a place Simone knew well. Since her mother's death from leukemia eighteen months ago, she'd become increasingly withdrawn from her friends. Being an only child, her father had thought it would do her good to spend time with close family, and had taken her to Gainesville regularly on weekends and holidays.

Her father had been right. Simone loved spending time at the unkempt house on Ridge Street, with its sprawling back garden that ran all the way down to the railway track. Her uncle's family was so warm to her, and she got on particularly well with her cousin Chloe. She hadn't spoken to them for over a week, not since her cell phone and the Internet went down, and while she had no idea if any of them were still alive, at least there was a chance.

The other reason for heading there was that she hoped there might still be fresh food. Gainesville was the poultry capital of America, and her uncle had worked for Fieldale Farms, the largest private employer in the city.

The job hadn't paid too well. "Wringing chickens' necks ain't much of living," Uncle Tyler said on more than one occasion with an ironic grin. Still, surely the survivors would have kept some of the processing plants going around the city? How hard was it to feed chickens? Driving down the center of the highway at seventy miles an hour, she would find out soon enough.

***

Ninety minutes later, she stopped for her first break. At a town called Northlake, she took the exit ramp where a gas station was signposted. She didn't need gas, but she did need to pee. Though she'd only passed three other travelers the whole time she was on the road—who'd all ignored her, and she, they—caution told her it was best to park somewhere off the highway for her rest stop.

She drove down the ramp where, at the bottom, she spotted a Shell station. At the junction, she turned into it and parked by the first pump. Gazing around, she saw that the station's window had been smashed, and snack foods and other items were strewn across the ground outside.

At the end pump, an old blue station wagon was parked. It appeared to have been abandoned. Someone must have been low on gas and pulled in here, she presumed. When they couldn't get the pumps going, they must have headed off on foot.

She dismounted the Honda and pulled out her Glock, then walked cautiously over to the vehicle. Peering in through the window, she confirmed it was unoccupied. No dead bodies inside. The back seat was stacked with cardboard boxes. Looking closer, she saw that they were laden with cans of food, boxes of spaghetti, packs of instant noodles, and chocolate bars.

Who on Earth would leave their food behind like that?

She was about to step away when a woman's shrill voice rang out. "Stop right there, mister! Move one inch and I'll blow you to pieces."

Simone froze. Still wearing her helmet and a motorcycle jacket, she realized the woman had mistaken her for a man. That only made the situation more dangerous.

"Drop that pistol on the ground," the woman ordered, her voice crackling harshly. "Real slow, you hear?"

Simone bent over and placed her Glock down on the forecourt's asphalt surface.

"All right, turn around."

Simone turned to see a woman step out from around the corner of the building, a double-barreled shotgun raised to her shoulder. Perhaps seventy years of age, she had squirrel-gray hair that was tied up in a bun, and wore a pair of faded dungaree overalls over a white cotton blouse. A pair of reading glasses dangled from a strap at her chest.

"D-don't shoot, ma'am," Simone said anxiously. "I'm not going to cause any trouble."

The woman took another step forward. Her bushy eyebrows scrunched up as she looked Simone up and down. "Is that a girl's voice I hear? Take off your helmet, dammit. Let me get a look at you."

Simone did as she was told, and lifted off her helmet.

"I'll be damned!" the woman exclaimed as Simone's dark curls cascaded to one side of her face. "Why, you don't look more than fifteen years old. Where the hell did you come from?"

"I'm from Charlotte. And I'll be sixteen in August."

The old lady took this all in. "Still no excuse to go stealing someone's food," she said sternly, keeping the shotgun pointed at Simone. "I wasn't gone more than a minute to take a pee around the back when I heard your motorcycle. Soon as I popped my head around the corner, there you were about to steal my stuff."

"I was just taking a look!" Simone protested. "I thought your car was abandoned." She gestured over to her motorbike. "I got my own food. I don't have room for any more."

"A likely story," the woman said with a snort. "Why would you think my car was abandoned? Can't you see I drove here to gas up?"

"Yes, ma'am. But the pumps don't work, not since the power went down. That's why I thought it got left here."

The old lady grimaced. "Can't say you're wrong there. Never occurred to me the pumps wouldn't work until I tried them."

A brief smile came over Simone's face. "Me too, the first time." She hesitated. "Ma'am, can I put my hands down now?"

The woman stared at her a moment, considering things. "I guess I can trust you. You seem sweet enough." She lowered the shotgun. "Go on, child. Pick up your gun."

"Thank you," Simone said gratefully. She stooped down and picked up her Glock, shoving it back inside her jacket pocket.

The old lady came over to the vehicle and rested her shotgun against the tailgate. "See? I trust you."

"Ma'am, where are you from?" Simone asked curiously. "And where you heading to?"

"I'm from a farm near Clemson, not more than fifteen miles from here. My husband, son, and his entire family died last week. I've been on my own for the past ten days."

"I'm sorry to hear that. How come you're alone? Did none of your neighbors survive?"

"A few of the smart ones did. Families that took precautions as soon as they found out what was going on. They barricaded themselves into their farms and wouldn't let anyone within five hundred yards of their properties. Last time I tried visiting one, they shot at me. Damn well nearly killed me too."

"Why?" Simone asked, puzzled. "You obviously aren't infected."

"They were worried I might be a carrier," the old lady explained. "There was talk on the radio that those who are immune to vPox can still spread the disease." She shrugged. "I guess I understand. They're just protecting their families. Still, it left me awful lonely. That's why I packed up and left today. Thought I'd better go search for some fellow survivors. You know, others like me, immune to this damned thing." She stared at Simone keenly. "How about you, child? What's your story?"

Simone took a deep breath before speaking. "I was living with my father when the pandemic started. After he died, I lived on the supplies I took from our local corner store. When I went out to get more, all the stores were empty and the supermarkets were under armed guard."

"Under armed guard? By who? The Army? The police?"

"No, by street gangs. And if you're not part of a gang, you don't eat. Simple as that."

The woman glanced over at Simone's motorbike. "So you joined one, I take it. Else you wouldn't have all that food you told me about, would you?"

Simone shook her head firmly. "I got my food the hard way. I wouldn't want to go through that again."

The woman stared at her. "For someone so young, you sure know how to take care of yourself."

Simone shrugged. "My father was a police officer. He taught me stuff. How to shoot, how to stay out of trouble, what to do if I got into it. I guess that's helped."

"I'll say. Tell me, where are you traveling to?"

"Gainesville. I have family there. I'm just praying some of them are still alive." Simone thought for a moment. "You can come with me if you want."

The old lady brightened at her proposition. "Sounds like a good plan. Trouble is…" She banged the roof of the station wagon with the flat of her hand. "I can't get no gas into this damned thing. Reckon I got enough to take me another twenty miles. That won't get me to Gainesville, that's for sure."

Simone pointed to her Honda. "My motorcycle is big enough to take both of us. How about you grab some food and spare clothes, and ride with me?"

The old lady stared at Simone, her eyes widening. Then she let out a loud cackle. "A teenager and an old granny riding the freeway on two wheels. That'll be a rare sight. All right, young lady. Count me in. It's not like I got much in the way of choices."

CHAPTER 12

At Camp Benton, Rollins had convened an emergency meeting. Sitting with him around the staffroom table were Bert Olvan, Mary Sadowski, and Henry Perter.

All four faces were creased with worry. Ninety minutes ago, after receiving Ned Granger's frantic radio message, Rollins and a group of eight men had rushed out of the camp in two pickups. Twenty minutes later, coming around a bend on the Sloans Gap Road, they'd encountered Granger's blue Nissan parked fifty yards ahead.

A devastating scene lay before them. Joe Meyer's motionless body slumped over the Nissan's bedside panel, while just yards away, Bob Harper lay sprawled face down in the grass. Both men were riddled with bullets. Approaching the vehicle, they discovered Marcus Welby inside the blood-splattered cabin.

Ned Granger was nowhere to be seen, and the men immediately commenced a search of the area. Rollins also radioed the North Cookson checkpoint, telling the guards to keep an eye out for Granger in case he was making his way back to the camp on foot.

After a fruitless thirty-minute search, two men picked up Bob Harper and placed him in the back of the Titan alongside Joe Macey. Then Marcus Welby was taken out of the cab and put in the back too. Leaving four men to continue the search for Granger, the rest of the group returned to Camp Benton.

On the way back, Rollins got on the radio again, with orders that no one was to leave the camp. He'd gotten in touch with both Cookson checkpoints and instructed them to return immediately. Their positions were far too exposed for a situation like this until he had a better idea of what was going on. Arriving back at camp, Rollins keyed in to the Wasson Lodge channel to inform Chris about the dismantling of the checkpoints, telling him to be on high alert for gang activity in the area.

Henry Perter leaned back in his chair and checked his watch for the umpteenth time. "Where the hell is he? It's been nearly two hours," he said worriedly. He and Granger had been close friends before the pandemic, and the strain of the situation was affecting him the most. His nervous disposition didn't help either. "If he escaped through the forest, he should have made it back by now."

"Unless he was too badly injured," Bert Olvan replied. "In which case…"

Mary Sadowski frowned. "You sure there was no sign of a blood trail leading anywhere?"

"We checked both sides of the road. There was blood leading up to the forest edge," Rollins responded, "a few feet past where Bob lay, then it just stopped."

Sadowski raised an eyebrow. "And?"

Rollins shrugged. No one at the camp was an expert tracker. It had been impossible to know exactly what had occurred during the shootout. "Maybe it was Bob's, and he turned back for some reason."

"Why would he do that?" Sadowski asked. "Anyway, didn't you tell me he was facing *in* the direction of the forest?"

Rollins nodded. "Perhaps he tried to surrender. Perhaps they kept shooting and he tried to run off again. The thing I don't understand is, why they were attacked in the first place? Nothing was taken. Not the truck, nor any weapons. It makes no sense."

"They must have bumped into a gang, and for whatever reason got caught up in a gunfight," Olvan said. "There's plenty of desperate people roaming the area these days. God knows I've seen enough of them myself on guard duty." He turned to Rollins. "By the way, John, withdrawing our men from the checkpoints was the smart thing to do. No point exposing them while there's people like that out there."

Since dismantling the checkpoints, Rollins had beefed up security on the camp perimeter. Five hundred yards up the camp driveway, Papa Three was no longer an observation point but a well-guarded checkpoint, and now the official entranceway in and out of Camp Benton.

Mary Sadowski, who had been staring off into the distance for the past minute, chose that moment to speak again. "There's another possibility. Something we haven't discussed yet."

All three men faced her.

"Go on," Rollins said. "What?"

"Maybe whoever killed our men took Ned with them."

There was a moment of stunned silence.

"Mary, why in hell's name would they do something like that?" Olvan asked incredulously.

Sadowski stared back at him. "For information, Bert. Maybe they're planning on taking this camp."

CHAPTER 13

Back at Old Fort, Mason and Russ sat at the garden table drinking beers. Inside the house and under guard, Tania was fixing up their prisoner's wounds. None were life threatening, so long as he didn't bleed to death. Once they learned all they could from him, Ned could bleed out all he liked as far as Mason was concerned. In fact, he might even help him out.

The group hadn't stayed long at the ambush point. Walking over to Ned, Russ had found a two-way radio lying in the grass nearby and told Mason they needed to move it, and fast. Four men dragged the sapling off the road, concealing it behind the tree line, then bundled their prisoner into the back of Mason's pickup, and raced all the way back to Old Fort.

Sipping on his beer, Mason thought for a moment about Russ. Sly, furtive, with a constant smirk on his lips, Mason had come to rely on him more and more since his arrival in the Cohutta. While at first it had simply been because he knew the area, it had quickly become more than that. Without a doubt, Russ was the smartest man on his crew, and his natural understanding of tactics was something Mason was increasingly becoming more reliant on.

As if reading his mind, Russ chose that moment to speak up. "I was thinking, Mason. Maybe we ought to make another trip to the lake before taking the lodge tonight."

"What for?"

"To make a hit and run on the sheriff's two roadblocks. Once we take the lodge, I doubt they'll keep them there. This might be our last chance to pick off some more of his men." Russ grinned. "Let's whittle them down to a stump."

Mason stared at him. "You know, for a scrawny little runt, you got a hell of a devious mind."

Russ smirked. "Us scrawny runts generally do."

"All right," Mason said with a chuckle. "This afternoon we'll take a crew back up there, see if we can't have a little more fun."

He stared up at the skies, where earlier a thick bank of rainclouds had drifted in from the east. It boded well for what was to come that evening. Poor visibility would favor the gang during their attack.

"Go fetch the map," he told Russ. "I want to go over the plan again. Once we take the lodge, then we can concentrate on Camp Benton, as Ned calls it. By the way, you'll need to work him hard. Make sure he gives up everything he knows about the place."

Russ grinned. "Don't worry, if need be I can always make a run into town for a blow torch and pliers," he joked. "That'll get him talking."

"Fetch them," Mason grunted. "He's a tough bastard. We're probably going to need them."

CHAPTER 14

The second leg of Simone's journey got off to a shaky start. Unaccustomed to her new companion's weight at the back, the initial takeoff out of the gas station lot caused the Honda to wobble dangerously.

"Slow down, dammit!" Marcie, as Simone learned her cantankerous friend was called, yelled in her ear. "You're going to get us both killed!"

Simone ignored her elder and better's advice. Instead, she pulled back on the throttle and the momentum from the powerful 250cc engine allowed the machine to right itself. Surprisingly, once they picked up speed on the highway, she found the motorbike no harder to ride than before.

It took under two hours for the pair to reach Gainesville. Arriving at the southern outskirts of the town, Simone took the exit for Route 129 that would take them through Pendergrass, Talmo, then into the city. Thinking about the countless times she and her father had driven here together made her choke up with emotion. She had to flip open her visor and wipe away the tears that had misted up her vision.

Fifteen minutes later, she passed the familiar Motel 6 on her right, then two hundred yards farther, drove under the I-985 overpass. Soon after, they arrived in the city center, where she swung right onto the deserted Jesse Jewell Parkway and headed north.

The city didn't have much in the way of fancy shopping options. Both sides of the highway consisted mainly of convenience stores, drugstores, discount stores, beauty supply stores, and grungy low-rise apartment blocks. Gainesville hadn't been an affluent town. One in three residents had never completed high school, and that included her uncle.

After a couple of miles, they reached the neighborhood of New Holland. A few blocks past the Baptist church, Simone turned onto Cornelia Street, then after a hundred yards took the first right onto Ridge Street.

At the top of the block she drew up beside a shabby, one-story, ranch style house. "Well, this is it," she said over her shoulder to Marcie.

In the driveway was a beat up pale blue Pontiac, and parked on the lawn an even older Ford pickup with more rust on it than paint.

Simone pointed over to them. "Those are both my uncle's cars. Looks like no one's left town."

Marcie stared at them dubiously. "I'm not so sure if that's a good sign." She clambered stiffly off the back seat and shrugged off her pack, placing it on the ground by the Honda's back wheel, while holding onto her shotgun, which she'd kept across her lap the entire journey. "All right child, let's go take a look. Just don't expect too much."

The two walked up the driveway past several folded metal chairs stacked to one side of the porch. Simone rapped lightly on the front door, then a second time. No one answered. The door was locked, the curtains drawn on both windows.

"Let's go around the back," she said, her heart beating fast.

With Marcie in tow, she trod up the narrow footpath that ran along the side of the house. At the end, a wooden gate led into the large, untidy garden. Passing through it, she spotted the metal swing where she used to push her cousin Brandon before chasing him around the overgrown shrubbery, and felt a lump in her throat. Everything looked the same as the last time she'd been here. That had been two months ago.

One thing had changed, though. Coming around the corner of the house, she stopped in her tracks. On the back lawn were three recent graves. Each had a wooden cross planted in the freshly dug earth.

Marcie came to a halt beside her. "I'm sorry," she said softly. "How many were in the family?"

"Four," Simone said in a tight voice. "My uncle and aunt, Chloe and…" she pointed to the smaller of the three graves, "Brandon. He was only seven."

That still left one more person. Someone strong enough to dig three graves.

"Wait there." Simone ran over to the back door. She turned the handle and it opened right away. Stepping inside, her heart sank as a familiar stench pervaded her senses, and she had to hold her nose to stop herself from gagging.

She walked through the kitchen, down the hall, and into the living room. Curled up in a fetal position on the couch was a fully dressed adult male. He wore muddy boots, his jeans caked in mud. Despite the ravaged and decomposing face, Simone recognized him instantly. With a sob, she turned around and ran back down the hall again.

Outside, Marcie stood waiting. She raised an eyebrow inquiringly. Simone shook her head, a feeling of despair descending over her. Though she'd known that the chance of finding any of her family members alive had been slim, the reality had suddenly and gruesomely been brought home to her. In the space of a couple of hours, Marcie had become the only living person she had any connection to in the entire world.

Neither one said anything for a while. Then Marcie said, "What do you want to do, child? I can help you clean up inside if you want to stay the night while we figure things out."

"There's nothing here for me except memories," Simone said resolutely. "We need to move on."

"All right. But where will we go? I don't know anywhere around here."

Simone composed herself. She took Marcie by the arm and started back down the side of the house. "Let's take a look around and see if we can find some fresh food. After all, this is Chicken Town, USA."

***

Ten minutes later, the two were driving north on I-985 and out of the city. Before leaving Ridge Street, Marcie explained to Simone that there was no point in checking out Gainesville's poultry processing plants. None of the chickens would be alive. Being a farmer herself, albeit not a poultry farmer, she knew how streamlined the production process was. It was a low-margin business that involved hatcheries, pullet, and breeder farms, all of which relied on feed such as corn and soy meal being transported to them regularly. That logistical supply chain had well and truly bitten the dust. If they wanted fresh food, they needed to find a regular farm.

Leaving New Holland behind them, they rode past a neighborhood known as White Sulphur Springs, then after a few miles crossed the tip of Lake Lanier over Clarks Bridge Road, heading north all the time.

Staring down at the lake, it occurred to Simone that there was another food source she hadn't considered up until now. Nestled in the Blue Ridge Mountains, Gainesville lay along the northeast shore of Lake Lanier, which was stocked with fish all year round. There spotted bass, bluegill, catfish, and various species of trout. She knew this because her father and uncle had been keen anglers, and though fishing as a sport had never appealed to her, to feed an empty belly was another matter entirely.

Crossing the bridge, they rode through beautiful countryside where woodland and open pastures lay to either side of the road, and thickets of oak and juniper dotted the landscape. They passed tractors and other mechanical equipment in the fields. Also paddocks, some with horses in them, others with cows.

"Somewhere here, there's got to be people. I'm sure of it." Marcie said excitedly in Simone's ear. "Slow down, dammit. You're driving too fast."

A few minutes later, shortly after passing a large manmade pond, Simone spotted movement. She brought the Honda to a halt and pointed across to an enclosed field on her left. "Look, Marcie. Over there!"

A tall figure wearing a short-sleeved blue shirt and sunglasses walked toward a large mansion nearby where a gray station wagon sat parked outside. He walked a little awkwardly. Ahead of him on a leash was a dog, perhaps a Golden Retriever. It was hard to tell at this distance.

Marcie shaded her eyes and squinted into the field. "My eyes ain't so good these days. What do you see?"

"There's a man walking his dog over to that house. I think he might be living there." Simone pointed up the road. "There's a gate ahead that leads down to it. What do you think? Shall we take a look?"

Marcie nodded. "Anything to get off this machine. We need to be careful though, especially after everything you told me about Charlotte. We don't know how many people are inside."

Butterflies formed in Simone's stomach as she slipped out the clutch and headed toward the gate. She prayed they had found somewhere safe. She really didn't want any more trouble.

CHAPTER 15

Crouched behind the bed, the barrel of his Remington 870 pump-action shotgun pointed toward the bedroom door, Billy Bingham strained his ears to catch the conversation of the intruders downstairs.

Two minutes ago, he'd heard the sound of motorcycle engines coming down the farm driveway. Alone in the house, he'd grabbed the shotgun and rushed upstairs moments before the front door burst open.

The farmhouse was small. With his bedroom door half ajar, the intruders' voices floated clearly up the stairs.

"Sheet, ain't there nothing to eat in this damned place?" a man said in a surly tone. "What kind of farm is this anyway?"

A second voice chuckled. "I told you, Josh. The sign outside says 'Willow Spring Organics.' This must have been one of those hippy dippy farms where the owners ate nothing but carrots and greens. You know how those tree huggers were."

"All that save the planet shit didn't stop them from dying off like flies, now did it?" the first man replied. "There are no safe spaces from vPox, especially if all you eat is rabbit food." There was the sound of kitchen drawers being thrown open. "Lookit, not even as much as goddamned egg in the house," the man said in disgust. "Maybe they kept a cellar here or something. What do you think?"

Billy's breath tightened. If the men found the pantry at the back of the kitchen, they'd find a lot more than just eggs, and he'd have to do something about that.

"Nah, come on, we're wasting time," the second man said impatiently. "There's plenty more places to check out around here. Somewhere they keep real food."

"I guess you're right." There was the sound of something crashing to the floor. "Damn tree huggers!"

"Quit bitching, Josh. They're dead, and a couple of no good drifters like us got the whole world to ourselves. Bet they never saw *that* coming."

The two men trudged back through the hall and the front door opened with a loud bang. Swiveling around to the window, Billy risked a peek outside.

Below in the yard, two men dressed in black leather jackets put their helmets on and climbed onto their machines. The engines came to life and they roared up the driveway. Passing through the gates, they turned onto the main road and disappeared from sight.

After the sound of their engines receded, Billy headed out of the room and down the stairs. He walked over to the front door and inspected it. The wood around the latch had been splintered off, but the hinges remained undamaged. With super glue and the screws his father kept in the work shed, he was sure he could fix it.

He closed the door and went down the hall into the kitchen. Strewn across the floor were half a dozen cheap plastic cups that had been used to plant herbs. Billy had been in the process of watering them when he'd heard the intruders arrive.

Squatting on his haunches, he cupped a hand on the floor and scooped the moist earth back into the cups, then replanted the basil, rosemary, and chive plants and placed them by the sink again. His mother had tended these plants, nurturing them until two days before she died. Billy had no intention of throwing them away.

He stared over at the pantry door on the far side of the room, thankful that he'd left a mop and bucket leaning against it. Perhaps that had been the reason the intruders hadn't bothered to check it out, mistaking it for a wall. Inside, stacked three deep, the shelves were laden with homemade canned meats, jars of various jams and pickled fruits, and at the back, sausages and hams hung from hooks on the ceiling, a treasure trove of culinary delights that would have made the intruders lick their lips.

If they had discovered the pantry, Billy would have had no choice but to come downstairs and confront them, and there was no way of knowing how that might have gone. Given that both men had pistols hanging from their waists, perhaps not very well.

He was grateful too that the men had been too lazy or disinterested to wander out the back door and into the farm itself. There they would have found plenty of livestock to get their hungry hands on. Willow Spring was a certified organic farm of fifteen acres. As well as chickens, the farm reared rabbits, duck, goats, and pigs, all fed on organic farm-grown material and GMO-free feeds.

Since the time he could walk, Billy's parents had involved him in the farm work, and he'd spent just about every day helping them out. He'd fed animals, built pens, planted seeds, and harvested vegetables that grew all year round, both in hoop houses and in the field.

Now his parents were dead, taken away a week ago by the terrible disease that had killed everyone he knew. In the space of just a few days, the longest days of his life, his idyllic world had been destroyed. Billy was only twelve years old.

***

For the first few days, no one in the neighborhood had been too concerned about the reports on TV and the Internet regarding the severe "flu" affecting the nation. In the remote hinterland of northern Georgia, people got on with their business. Chicken farms continued to breed broilers for the processing plants in Gainesville, and in the fields, farmers tended their crops.

The first thing Billy knew about the problem was when he arrived home from school one day to see his father in the kitchen, pale-faced and distraught. Normally at that time of year, it was his mother who was there to greet him while his father worked outdoors. Lately he'd been busy harvesting fava beans and asparagus that he grew in two large polytunnels.

"Dad, what's wrong?" he asked, observing his father's grim countenance. He looked out the kitchen window and into the garden where his mother often worked when he got back from school. "Where's Mom?"

"Your mother's not well. She's upstairs in bed."

The previous day, when Billy returned from school, his mother had complained of a headache. Her eyes had been watery and her face blotchy. By early evening, she'd gone to bed and he hadn't seen her that morning.

"Does she have the same thing as my classmates?" he asked. "Some of them came to school today with rashes on their faces. Mr. Glendon sent them all home."

"Yes, the same thing." His father hesitated a moment. "I'm sure she'll be fine in a couple of days, but until this thing blows over, maybe its best you stay at home. That okay with you?"

Billy grinned, delighted with the news. Though he didn't hate school, like any other kid he jumped at any excuse not to attend. Besides, his closest friend, Jimmy Cartwright hadn't been in class for the previous two days, another good reason not to go.

"Sure. You want me to help you in the hoop house after lunch?"

His father wiped his brow. "Thanks, Billy, I could do with some help. I've been feeling a little under the weather myself lately."

Billy dumped his schoolbag on a chair and headed out of the room.

"Where are you going?" his father asked sharply.

Billy wheeled around. "To see Mom."

"Not now, son, she's sleeping. Maybe you can see her later tonight." He gestured to Billy. "Help me make lunch. You have any idea where the mayo is? I have no idea where your mother keeps anything around here."

That evening Billy got to see his mother. After dinner, while his father was in the living room, he crept up the stairs and into his parents' bedroom. Crossing over to the bed, he looked down at her.

Barely able to believe his eyes, he jerked his head back. His mother's normally thick brown hair had thinned dramatically, and her face was covered in ugly, pus-filled blisters. Blood oozed out of her nose, and though asleep, her mouth was twisted in a painful grimace.

"Mom!" he gasped. He reached down and shook her shoulder.

His mother stirred, struggling to crack open her eyes. In horror, Billy saw they were completely bloodshot, and a gluey pink liquid leaked out of both corners. She didn't appear to recognize him, and closed them again.

"Mom, wake up!"

His mother tried one more time, this time managing to stay awake a moment. "Billy…" she croaked. "Stay away."

Tears welled up in his eyes. "Mom…please."

Despite his urgings, his mother closed her eyes and didn't open them again. In a state of shock, Billy ran downstairs and into the living room to see his father lying on the sofa shivering uncontrollably. On his face were the beginnings of the raised lumps he'd first seen on his mother a day ago.

"Dad!" he cried out. "What's going on?"

"Billy, not now. I need to sleep," his father wheezed. "Go fetch me a blanket, I'm cold."

Billy couldn't understand it. It was mid-June, early evening on what had been a sweltering summer's day. Nonetheless, he fetched his father a blanket. By the time he returned, his father was asleep. Covering him, Billy sat down on the armchair next to him and started to cry. Something deep inside told him that his world was unraveling, that it would never be put back together again.

The following morning, he hadn't dared go in see his mother, and had hurried downstairs and into the living room.

His father's condition had deteriorated. The raised lumps had become pus-filled, and his eyes were glassy and unfocused. "Billy, come here," he gasped, raising his head off the cushion.

Billy walked over to the sofa. His father stared him up and down. "Are you feeling okay?" he asked. "Do you have a headache, chills? Tell me the truth now."

"No," Billy answered.

His father lowered his head. "Thank God. You must be one of the few that's immune to this thing." He leaned forward again, his brow glistening with sweat. "Listen to me good, Billy. This fever everyone is coming down with, it's real bad. I've been reading about it on the Internet. Before it's done, it's going to kill a lot of people."

Billy's eyes widened. "What do you mean? Are you and Mom going to…?"

His father hesitated. "You've been to see your mother, haven't you?"

Billy nodded.

"Then you know how bad this is. It's happening all across the nation. Emergency services are failing everywhere. I took your mother to the hospital in Gainesville yesterday, that's how I know. I couldn't even get her in the door."

"Dad, Mom looks terrible. Are you going to get like that too?"

His father averted his eyes. "Maybe. Look, Billy, if we don't make it, you're going to have to take care of things by yourself for a while, you understand? There'll be no one to help you."

Billy's lower lip trembled. He had never felt such utter terror his entire life.

His father reached out and shook his shoulder gently. "When we're gone, you have to take our bodies outside. It's not good to keep them in the house. Put us in the cart and take us up to the new ditch. The one I built the oth—"

"Dad!" Billy screamed, putting his hands over his ears. "Stop!"

The other week, his father had rented an excavator and built a drainage ditch alongside an unused field at the back of the farm, one that tended to flood each winter. Previously it had been used only for grazing, and his father wanted to put it to better use.

"Fetch the diesel can from the shed, then burn our bodies."

By this stage, Billy was sobbing wildly, his head resting on his father's chest.

His father stroked his hair. "Billy, leaving us in the house will only cause disease. You have to do this."

"I can't!" Billy wailed. "Why can't I just go to Jimmy's house?"

The Cartwrights lived seven miles from the Binghams. Billy's parents often dropped him over to their house on the weekends and vice versa.

"They're going through the same thing as us."

"Is Jimmy okay?"

"No." His father turned away with a tired sigh. "You better let me sleep. We'll talk again later."

Numb inside, Billy stood up and left the room. When he reached the door, his father called out to him. "Billy, you're going to have to grow up fast. Just remember everything I've taught you and you'll do fine."

It was the last coherent conversation he had with his father. Two days later, following his instructions, he dragged his parents' bodies out of the house, then one at a time, hauled them in a cart up to the ditch, doused them with diesel fuel, and set their carcasses alight. Sobbing, he'd turned away and ran back to the house.

His father had been right. Billy was growing up fast. It wasn't like he had a lot of choice.

CHAPTER 16

Outside the mansion, Simone stood beside Marcie at the top of the porch steps where above the door, a wooden sign spelled: Zephyr House. To one side of the building, a ground floor window had been smashed. Simone guessed it was how the man in the blue shirt had first gotten inside.

The Honda stood parked in the driveway, facing in the direction of the gates in case they needed to cut and run in a hurry. Simone wondered exactly how fast that would be for Marcie at seventy-three years of age. She hoped she didn't need to find out anytime soon.

She rapped the door knocker a couple of times in quick succession, firmly, though not so hard that it would appear aggressive. Moments later, there was the sound of footsteps in the hall and some muffled talking.

"There's at least two of them," Marcie whispered, clutching her shotgun tightly. "Careful."

The footsteps got closer, and a gruff voice called out from behind the door, "Who's there? And what do you want?"

Marcie gestured to Simone to speak. "Sorry to disturb you, mister," she said in her most polite voice. "It's just we were passing by and saw you in the field."

"And?"

"And?" Marcie spluttered indignantly beside her. "Seeing as there's practically no one left in the whole damned world, we thought we'd drop by and say hello. But if you're not feeling sociable, we'll go and make friends elsewhere. No skin off our noses." She turned to leave. "Come on, Simone. No point in wasting time here."

"Wait!" a second voice called out. It was that of a younger man. Simone guessed it was the one she'd seen in the field earlier. There was the sound of shuffling feet. A bolt slid across, the latch unlocked, and the door opened a couple of inches.

"Push," the voice said.

Marcie's right eyebrow arched. "What in tarnation are these people playing at?" she muttered. She leveled her shotgun and gestured for Simone to open the door. Simone stepped forward and gave it a shove, then stepped quickly back again.

The door swung open to reveal two men in the hallway. One was an old man in a wheelchair with gray hair and an unkempt beard. Behind him stood the tall man in the short-sleeved blue shirt and sunglasses. He was younger, fortyish, and gripped both handles of the wheelchair.

Simone stared down at the old man and gasped. In the grip of his gnarled and bony hands was a double barrel shotgun pointed straight at her.

The old man gasped as well. He too stared down both barrels of a 12 gauge shotgun, the one Marcie held up to her shoulder.

"Goddammit!" he exclaimed.

For one awful moment, Simone was convinced one of the two was about to open fire.

"Fred, is everything okay?" the younger man asked nervously.

Studying him further, Simone understood the situation. "Everything is fine," she said soothingly. "I'm Simone, from Charlotte. This is my friend Marcie. Don't worry, she's actually very nice."

"Then what's she doing pointing that gun at me?" Fred said angrily. "Nothing nice about that."

Marcie snorted. "Same could be said for you, mister. That's no way to greet a friendly face."

"Lady, ain't nothing friendly about your face," Fred replied, scowling. He shifted his gaze to Simone. "As for you, now that's a different matter." He sighed. "All right, no point in us pointing these damned things at each other. Someone is bound to get hurt." Lowering his shotgun, he rested it on the blanket across his knees. A moment later, Marcie followed suit.

Simone breathed a sigh of relief. She stared up at the younger man, still gripping the wheelchair and looking around uncertainly. "Pardon me for asking, but is your friend blind?"

Fred nodded. "Eric is blind as a bat. Me, I'm crippled from the waist down. On our own, we're pretty much hopeless, but together we make a hell of a team." He made an impatient gesture. "Well, no point standing there like a couple of goons, you may as well come inside. Eric, turn this thing around. Back to the kitchen!"

With a deft shuffle of his feet, Eric made a one-eighty turn and headed down the hall. "Bolt the door after you!" Fred yelled out over his shoulder. "We don't want any unwanted visitors getting in. Been there, done that already."

Marcie gave Simone an indifferent shrug, then stepped into the house. Simone followed her inside, locked the door securely, and followed her down the hall.

At the end, she entered a large and tastefully decorated kitchen. The walls were covered floor to ceiling with white wooden panels, and on one side were huge cabinets with carved moldings and fluted corners. Over by the window was a long granite countertop with a large porcelain sink centered in it. Whoever had lived here before had had money, that was for sure.

The Golden Retriever Simone had seen in the field earlier came over to her. It looked up at her with warm brown eyes and wagged its tail gently. She guessed it was a guide dog.

"Say hello to our guests, Molly," Fred said as Simone reached down to stroke the dog's head. "That's Simone. She's the nice one."

There was the smell of freshly brewed coffee in the room. On a rustic-looking oak table in the corner were two mugs and a half-full coffeepot.

Fred caught Marcie staring at it. "Either of you want coffee?" he asked. "We were just having some when you arrived."

"No thank you." Simone loved the smell of coffee, but hated the taste.

"I'd murder one," Marcie said. "Haven't had a real coffee in over a week. With everything that's been going on, it feels more like a year."

Fred wheeled himself over to a marble-topped island in the middle of the room. On it was a wooden tray with several mugs in it. He grabbed one, wheeled back to the table, and poured out a drink for Marcie. Taking it from him, she dolloped out two heaped spoons of brown sugar, stirred them in, and took an eager sip.

Fred gestured over to a mason jar on the countertop, a quarter full with ground coffee. "We got enough for a few more days, then it's back to the instant again." He wrinkled his nose in distaste. "Not looking forward to that."

Using his hands, Eric edged his way over to the far side of the table and picked up his mug.

"How long have you two known each other?" Simone asked.

"Not long. A few days."

"Are you both from Gainesville?"

"No," Fred replied, "Maysville. It's close by."

Across the table Eric smiled gently. "I don't think the survivors thought too much of us there, did they, Fred? They sure left us behind pretty quick. So much for small town manners."

Fred chuckled. "If only they thought of pairing us together, maybe they'd have taken us with them. We did a good job chasing off those no good varmints the other day. Sent them packing with their tails between their legs."

"What happened?" Simone asked, remembering Fred's comment in the hallway.

"Two days ago a group of men tried to break in here, looking to steal our food," Eric explained. "I had to run around like crazy, pushing Fred from one room to another while he blasted away at them through the windows."

Fred grinned. "Hard left, full ahead! Turn right! Stop! Peppered a couple of them with buckshot before they got the message, that's for sure."

"So that's how come the front window is broken," Simone said.

"Right." A worried look flashed across Fred's face. "God knows what will happen when the last of our food runs out. It's one thing warding off people trying to steal our supplies, another thing hunting for our own food out there."

Simone understood what he meant. Confined to a wheelchair, hunting was out of the question for Fred. Being blind, it would be impossible for Eric too. Life would soon become harsh for the two men.

"We saw plenty of lakes and rivers on our way here. Did you choose this area so you could fish?"

A thin smile came to Fred's lips. "Smart girl. Yes, we were planning something along those lines. Back when I had the use of my legs, this area used to be my old stomping ground. I know it like the back of my hand. So long as Eric can get me down to the riverbank, we should be okay."

Marcie's bushy eyebrows knitted together. "But why stay here?" she asked. "Surely it makes more sense to live at a farm where some of the livestock have survived."

Fred looked at her sternly. "Do you have any idea how hard it was for us to even make it this far? And what use exactly is a farm to us? You think me and Eric plan on milking the cows each morning, or chasing sheep in the field?"

At the far end of the table, Eric chuckled. "We're good, but we're not that good."

A thought occurred to Simone. "Pardon me, but how *did* you get here? I mean, neither of you can drive."

"A minor miracle, that's how," Fred replied. "Eric got in behind the wheel and operated the pedals of that old station wagon you saw parked outside. I sat beside him and steered."

Simone shook her head in amazement. "Wow."

"To be honest, with no cars on the road, it wasn't as hard as you might think. Though we did have a couple of close shaves along the way."

"So what now?" Marcie asked. "You two plan on living here on your own?"

"No choice," Eric said flatly, staring sightlessly at her through his dark glasses. "So far, the only folk interested in us want to rob us blind." He chuckled at his little joke. "It's a dog eat dog world out there. No one has shown any intention of letting us into their lives."

Marcie sighed. "I know how that feels. No one wanted to take me in either, until I met this sweet little girl," she added, glancing over at Simone.

"Well, as far as I'm concerned, you're both welcome to stay here," Eric said. "If that's okay with you, Fred?"

Fred nodded. "Absolutely. Having a little help wouldn't go amiss." He paused a moment. "Before we left Maysville, we stocked up with plenty of seeds from a gardening store. It's not too late in the season to grow vegetables. All it takes is a bit of elbow grease."

Simone grinned. "You're just looking for someone to dig you a vegetable bed, aren't you?"

Sipping his coffee, Eric laughed. "Fred plans on putting me to work in the garden. I can use a spade pretty well, so long as someone points me in the right direction."

"So, how about it? Will you stay?" Fred asked, staring first at Simone, then Marcie. Despite his casual tone, Simone could sense the underlying desperation. Without any help, a bleak future awaited the pair. She looked at Marcie questioningly.

Marcie took another slurp from her coffee, then set her mug down on the table. "I guess we can stay awhile. It's not like we got someplace in particular to be." She looked at Fred with a wry smile. "I've grown my own vegetables for this past forty years. Don't worry, we'll get something going in your garden."

***

That evening, as the last of the summer light faded from the kitchen window, Simone and Marcie headed off to bed. Hauling their gear up the stairs, they found the master bedroom at the back of the house. Since they'd arrived, neither Fred nor Eric had ventured upstairs. "I can't get up there, and not much point in Eric going if he can't see a damned thing," Fred had commented. "I'm pretty sure there's no dead bodies in the rooms or we would have smelled them by now."

Marcie ran her flashlight around the bedroom, a high-ceilinged, cream-colored room with thick purple drapes drawn across the windows. On one wall was a wood-framed mirror, while on the other side was an elegant Shaker-style wardrobe.

The bed was large, and had a carved wood headboard. It was fully made up, with fresh sheets and a multi-colored throw on top. Simone breathed a sigh of relief to see no dead person in it. There was always the chance a decomposing body might have lain under the blankets.

"What do you think, child? You want to sleep on your own?" Marcie asked. She aimed her flashlight back toward the door. "In which case, we better check out another room for you."

Simone shook her head. "It's creepy up here. Let's sleep together."

"All right." Marcie cracked a smile. "But I got to warn you, I tend to snore at night. Used to drive my husband mad. If I wake you up, you have my permission to turn me over onto my side. That's what Dan used to do, God bless him. It usually does the trick."

Simone giggled. "Okay, I'll remember that."

Marcie frowned at her. "You don't fart in your sleep, do you? Dan used to do that, especially when he ate too much. I used to kick him out and make him sleep in the spare room."

"As far as I know, I don't," Simone laughed. "All right, fair is fair. If I fart during the night, you have my permission to kick me out of the bed. I'll go sleep in the corner."

Marcie began laughing too. "I'm so glad we met at the gas station today. It was a blessing. Nearly sixty years between us, yet we get on famously." She sighed. "The world's turned into a strange place, that's for darn sure. Something tells me that ain't going to change anytime soon."

CHAPTER 17

At 3:10 a.m., a group of heavily-armed men piled into four pickup trucks and left the town of Old Fort. Thirty minutes later, the convoy arrived at Devil's Point, on the southern shores of Lake Ocoee. A little over a mile away lay Wasson Lodge, the focus of their attention that evening.

The night was moonless. Not a star could be seen in the skies above, and a light drizzle sprayed across Mason's face as he got out of his vehicle. Perfect conditions for the task at hand.

With Russ leading the way, the men entered the forest and walked single file along a narrow trail. Twenty minutes later, Russ stopped and raised his hand. He pointed ahead to where two pine trees stood directly opposite each other on the trail.

"Tripwire," he said in a hushed tone when Mason reached him. Stepping forward, he took out his knife and cut the fishing line set at ankle height between the two trees. After he'd dragged the ends to either side of the path, the group continued forward.

Soon, they reached the edge of the forest by a large clearing. A hundred yards away, barely visible in the gloom, they could make out the silhouette of the lodge.

Russ pointed over to it. "Behind the house is the field that backs onto the lake," he whispered. "That's where their trailers are parked."

"You're sure no one is staying inside the lodge?" Mason whispered back.

Russ shook his head.

"All right, let's do this."

Mason gave the signal, and his men split into two teams. From the sketch Russ had drawn previously, he knew that guard posts had been placed on either side of the lodge. The plan was to attack both posts simultaneously, then continue on to the trailers.

Creeping along the side of the forest, Mason and his men started toward the east gable end, while Russ's team headed over to the opposite side of the building.

A few minutes later, Mason came to within fifty feet of a sandbag parapet and halted his men. Gazing through the inky darkness, it was hard to tell whether the post was manned or not. He selected two men and headed deeper behind the tree line. Treading softly through the forest, they reemerged twenty feet behind the guard post.

Mason squinted, and could make out a slumped figure sitting on a stool, his head resting on top of the sandbags. He leveled his rifle and strode forward, a man to either side of him.

The guard didn't wake up until Mason was almost on top of him. With a start, he stood up and reached for his rifle. Mason pulled the trigger of his Heckler & Koch AR-15 style carbine and fired off several rounds in quick succession. The guard staggered back and toppled over the stack of sandbags.

From the other side of the lodge came the sound of more gunfire. It stopped almost as soon as it started. Russ had taken out the second guard post.

Mason called out to the rest of his men who'd lain in wait by the forest edge, out of the field of fire. All eight spread out across the short grass, and jogged over to a row of four trailers parked fifty yards away.

By that time, shouts of alarm started to come from inside them. The door to the nearest trailer flung open and a figure stepped out. "Tim! James! What's going on?" a man's voice called out.

Mason opened fire. The man stumbled down the steps and fell to the ground. Striding forward, Mason shone his flashlight down to see a blond-haired man wearing a pair of sports shorts lying motionless on the ground. A round had hit him above the right eye, and blood seeped out of the wound. Mason kicked his rifle away. Pointing to the open door, he ordered his men to check if anyone else was inside.

Out of the corner of his eye, he spotted a figure emerging from the last trailer. It began to creep away. Mason opened fire again. Immediately, the figure sprinted around the back of the trailer and disappeared from view.

Just then, Russ and the rest of his men arrived, sprinting across the field. In a matter of seconds, all four trailers were surrounded front and back. No one else dared come out of any of them.

Mason walked up to the second trailer. He gave the side several hard raps with the butt of his rifle. "Open the door and throw your weapons out!" he yelled. "That way no one else gets hurt."

A moment later, the door opened. Mason heard the sound of several thuds in the grass. "That's all the guns I got!" a woman's frightened voice called out.

"All right. Come on out!" Mason angled his flashlight at the door and a stocky woman with short gray hair came down the steps. Blinking in the harsh glare of his torch, she threw her hands in the air. "Anyone else inside?"

The woman shook her head. She stared over toward the first trailer, and let out a groan when she spotted the man lying motionless outside.

Mason gestured for one of his men to check the woman's trailer. The crew member strode past her and went up the steps. He peeked his head around the door, then went inside. A moment later, he came back out again. "All clear, boss."

The last two trailers were cleared in the same manner. At the end of the process, only two people stood outside.

"We're missing someone," Russ said, frowning. "There should be six to account for altogether."

"One guy ran off earlier," Mason told him. "No big deal."

He walked over to the two figures, the second of which was a stockily-built man in his thirties. "You!" he barked at him. "Are you the leader of this sorry group?"

"No. Not me," the man replied, shaking badly.

"Then who? The guy that ran away?"

The man pointed over to the figure lying sprawled in the grass by the first trailer. "Chris. That's him over there."

"So, who are you then?"

"I'm Eddy. I'm…uh…in charge of camp security."

"Well you did a piss poor job of it, didn't you?" Mason chuckled. "All right, where did Walter go after he left here?"

Eddy looked at him in surprise. "You know Walter?"

"Yeah, I know Walter. Where did he go?"

"I-I have no idea."

Mason's hard eyes bore into Eddy's. "Why the fuck not?"

"We didn't leave on good terms. Him and his group just up and left."

Mason spat on the ground. "You're no use to anyone, are you? No information…lousy security." He reflected a moment. "In Roman times, if a general conducted himself badly in battle, afterward he'd fall on his sword. It was the honorable thing to do. Eddy, are you an *honorable* man?"

"I…uh…I don't know."

"I'm taking that as a *no*." Mason withdrew the Sig Sauer P226 pistol holstered by his waist and leveled it at Eddy. "Guess you leave me no choice."

To the sound of hysterical screams from the woman, Mason fired two shots into Eddy's chest. With a gasp, he fell to the ground in a crumpled heap.

"*No!*" the woman wailed. "You promised no one else would get hurt."

Mason holstered his weapon. "Sorry, lady, I lied. What you got to understand is, this is a 'take no prisoners' situation we got here."

Russ sniggered. "That's right. Ain't no Geneva Convention to tell us different either. Come to think of it, ain't no Geneva, period."

He stared coldly at the woman, who'd fallen to her knees and was weeping uncontrollably. "What you plan on doing with her, Mason? She's too damned old and ugly to give to the men."

Mason looked down at the woman. "Stand up!" he yelled at her. "Run like hell. If you're still here in ten seconds, I'll shoot you down like a dog."

CHAPTER 18

Rollins dreamed of his wife and daughter. It was not a pretty dream. During waking hours, he managed to keep their painful memories at bay. While he slept, however, his mind was defenseless, the horror seeped in, and he awoke most nights calling out their names.

This time he woke up to the distant crackle of gunfire. It sounded too far away to have come from anywhere near the camp. Perhaps it came from somewhere down on the Cookson Creek Road? He checked his watch: 4:05 a.m. Reaching over to the bedside table, he grabbed his radio.

"Papa Three, this is Bravo One. Do you read me? Over," he said, contacting the guard manning the new checkpoint placed across the camp's driveway.

"*Bravo One, read you loud and clear, over,*" came the reply a few seconds later.

"I heard gunfire. Where is it coming from? Over."

"*Can't tell for sure, Sheriff. Sounds like it came from the lodge. Maybe they had to chase some people away, over.*"

Relieved it hadn't been an intruder trying to break into their camp, Rollins instructed the guard to stay vigilant, then signed off. About to go back to sleep, he thought of something.

He got out of bed and padded across the cabin in his bare feet to where a second radio, the one keyed into the Wasson Lodge frequency, sat on the kitchen table.

"Chris, this is Sheriff Rollins, do you read me? Over," he said, pressing down on the PTT button.

There was no reply. He tried to get through several more times without reply, then made one last attempt before giving up. "Chris, I heard gunshots over your way. Everything all right? Over."

There was a crackle of static, then a gruff low-toned voice came over the channel, one Rollins didn't recognize. *"Sheriff, Chris can't take your call right now, on account of he's dead. Anything I can help you with? Over."*

Rollins's eyes widened. "Dead? What the hell you talking about?" he blurted out, not bothering with the proper radio formalities.

"Dead, as in departed. No longer with us. That goes for the rest of his people too."

Rollins's head spun. "Who am I talking to?" he asked, desperately trying to muster his thoughts.

"This is Mason, your friendly new neighbor." In the background there was the sound of another man sniggering. Then the first man's voice came back on. *"Tell you what, Sheriff. How about in the morning, you and me find someplace where we can talk? That sound good to you?"*

"No it doesn't," Rollins snarled. "I'll have nothing to do with a murderer."

"Aw, don't be like that. I have a friend of yours staying with me you might want to say hello to, over."

Rollins's pulse quickened. This was the same group that had attacked Ned and his men earlier that afternoon. He was thankful he'd withdrawn the guards from the Cookson Road checkpoints. Perhaps they would be dead right now if he hadn't. "If you've got Ned, I need to speak to him now, over," he said in a tight voice, controlling his emotions.

"Ned's not with me at the moment, but you can say hello to him tomorrow."

"He better be okay, you sonofabitch," Rollins said through gritted teeth.

There was a dry laugh on the line. *"I wouldn't say he's feeling great, but hey, he's alive. Whether he stays that way or not depends on you."*

"What the hell's that supposed to mean?"

"We'll talk about it tomorrow. I'll contact you in the morning to arrange details. Goodnight and sweet dreams, Sheriff. Over and out."

With that the radio went dead, leaving Rollins to stare out the window into the dead of night.

CHAPTER 19

The two hunters left camp at dawn. In the dim morning light, a bleary-eyed Cody followed Clete up a narrow trail leading into the hills. Reaching the first ridgeline, he stared down at where their trailers were parked in the valley below and spotted his cream and white KZ Sportsman.

Inside, Emma lay in bed, sound asleep. Fifteen minutes ago, Clete had rapped lightly on Cody's door. He'd climbed out of bed without disturbing her, and quickly got dressed. As per Clete's instructions of the previous evening, he took no gear with him, only his Kimber 1911 by his right hip, his buck knife on the other, a compass, water bottle, and a couple of energy bars stuffed into his shorts. They weren't going far. Clete had scouted out a good location to set their traps only a couple of miles away from the camp.

With the Tennessean leading the way, they dropped over the far side of the ridge and headed in the direction of Jacks River Falls. After twenty minutes of hard hiking, the trail brought them to a large hollow covered by thick woodland.

Clete drew to a stop and pointed a finger. "Ahead is a game trail that leads down into the gully. It's a perfect place to set our traps."

"How many did you bring with you?" Cody asked.

"None. I'm going to teach you how to make them."

Cody grinned. "We going to make snares?"

"Nope. Snares aren't much good for catching anything bigger than rabbits or squirrels. I want to show you a method how to catch medium-sized game or even larger."

"Why can't we use snares for them too?"

"It's hard to set one powerful enough to lift a larger animal off the ground," Clete explained. "Generally speaking, with a snare you're going to get a body catch. If you can't get the animal off the ground, it's just going to chew out of the snare. Don't matter what type of cordage you're using, a desperate animal is going to chew right through it. You have to use a steel snare, and right now I don't have any of them."

"So, what sort of trap we going to make?"

"We're making a windlass trap. That's a killing trap, and a dead animal don't chew out of nothing. Today we're just going to build a small one, suitable for a rabbit or squirrel. But it's the exact same principle for a larger animal too."

Cody followed Clete along the game trail that first ran across some high ground before dipping down to a tiny stream at the bottom of the hollow. Halfway down, Clete stepped away from the trail and headed over to where a thicket of white pine saplings grew on one side. Finding two skinny ones standing close together, he dropped to one knee and waved Cody over.

"All right. Here is where we're going to build our machine."

"Machine?"

Clete nodded. "It's a means of harnessing power us humans have used for centuries." He winked at Cody. "You'll see. It's really very simple."

Shrugging his pack off his back, he opened it up, rummaged inside, and took out a short length of wood about a quarter-inch in diameter. Hammered through one end was a three-inch nail. It was bent slightly inward, almost like a hook.

At the other end, the piece of wood had been carved out to create a flat, narrow surface.

"Took me all of two minutes to make this." Catching Cody's expression, Clete added, "Don't worry, kid, you're going to make one soon enough. First of all, let me demonstrate how this works."

Searching his pack again, he took out a length of bank line and wrapped it around the two trees about a foot off the ground, then tied it up.

He held up the piece of wood with the nail in it. "With enough force, this sixteen penny nail will drill through the back of a critter's head and kill it stone cold dead." He pointed to the cord between the two trees. "And this windlass here is going to create that force."

Inserting the tapered end of the stick, the end without the nail, he pushed it between the wrapped cord all the way down to the stop cut. He began to wind it up, twisting the piece of wood around and around again.

It dawned on Cody exactly how the windlass worked. "The tension in the line is going to power the nail, isn't it?" he said. "Kind of like a propeller wound by an elastic band on a model airplane."

"You got it, kid. When this thing gets tripped, the nail is going to spin a half rotation and hit the animal in the back of its head. It's got to be wound good and tight, though."

After a few more rotations, Clete stopped. "Take this while I go find me the trigger."

Fascinated by the deadly simplicity of the weapon, Cody held it in place, feeling the tension in the wound-up bank line. Clete walked over to a nearby willow tree about twenty feet away. Selecting a branch, he snapped off a foot-long twig and came back over. He squatted beside Cody again and took out his Leatherman.

"It takes a lot of practice to build this peg trigger," he warned. "Watch carefully."

With his knife, he made two deep cuts in the stick, about an inch and a half from each end, then made a third cut dead center on the opposite side. Placing his thumbs to either side of the middle notch, he bent the wood back gently, forcing it to peel all the way down to the notch at one end.

Snapping it off, he held it up to Cody. "This here is the post stick." Going through the same motion on the remaining piece, he then sharpened the end to a point. "And this is the bait stick."

Taking over the windlass from Cody again, he held the post stick perpendicular to the ground, then deftly latched the bait stick onto it with the sharpened point sticking out. Gently, he lowered the windlass on top of it.

He slowly took both hands away. The trap stayed intact, the tension from the windlass holding everything in place.

Clete sat back on his heels and grinned. "Perfect. Next animal to nose its way up here is going to feel its ears burn in a hurry."

"Don't we have to bait the stick?"

"Sure." Clete gestured over to his pack. "I got some peanut butter that'll bring the next passing squirrel over in a hurry."

"What's squirrel taste like?" Cody asked. "Somebody once told me they taste pretty rank."

Clete shrugged. "Depends on how many days you've gone without eating. Personally, I like 'em. I gut and skin them, then leave them to hang a couple of days. If you rub some salt and spice in, and chuck them on a wood grill, they've always tasted pretty good to me. 'Course, just about anything tastes good with enough smoke, garlic, and jalapenos. Like I said, you can scale this trap up to kill a small hog or deer. That's what I call a varied diet to get you through the winter."

"Really? A large stick is enough to kill a hog?"

"Sure, if it's sharp enough, and wound right. Deer antler is pretty good too." Clete reached into his pack again and pulled out the bank line along with another sixteen penny nail. "Your turn. Let's see how good you are."

***

Under Clete's guidance, Cody soon built three more traps. Once he'd gotten the hang of it, he was amazed how quickly they could be made. First, he found a length of wood to carve out the windlass sticks, and hammered a nail through each one. The peg triggers were trickier, but after a few unsuccessful attempts, he finally got the hang of them too.

The hardest part was the actual setting of the trigger. At first, he found it impossible to get the bait stick to balance on the post stick; it kept sliding off. Clete instructed him to rough up the bottom of the sticks so that there was enough friction to keep them from slipping. Soon after, he was up and running, and found that by balancing the bait stick at about a twenty-five-degree angle, he could position the windlass on top of the post stick easily.

During the process, Clete taught him a few more tricks, like to make sure to use extra bank line to fasten the windlass securely; if an animal didn't die instantly, you didn't want it to destroy the trap and escape. Also, how to build a funnel using stones and dead wood around the trap so that the animal approached it head on. Everything he taught was logical and simple, learned from decades of hunting experience. Every trick, every refinement, improved the percentage chance of trapping an animal.

Finally, baiting all four traps with peanut butter, they set off back to the camp. It was 8 a.m., and they wanted to get back in time to see Pete, Ralph, and Maya off before they left on their recruitment mission. That evening, they would check the traps. In the summer heat, any dead animal would go bad quickly.

"You done good, kid," Clete said as they hiked back up the hill. "Never saw someone figure out how to make those peg triggers as quick as you. You got a God-given talent for this shit."

Grinning, Cody said, "Only 'cos I've got a great teacher."

Clete chuckled. "Better wait till we catch something before you say that. Next time I'll show you how to make a box trap for catching pheasant. Mmm-mmm! I just love me some roast pheasant!"

CHAPTER 20

Mason sat at a camping table outside his new trailer sipping coffee. Earlier that morning he'd gotten Tania to dump out Chris's belongings from the slide-out wardrobe and cabinets, replacing them with their own. The thirty-five-foot Highland Ridge Roamer was far roomier than the trailer he'd hauled up from Knoxville two days ago. It seemed a shame to let it go to waste.

It was a beautiful day. The cloudy weather of the past twenty-four hours had dissipated, and a bright June sun shone down from the skies. Earlier that morning, he'd dispatched a detail to Old Fort with orders to drive up all his crew's trailers. Around the camp, his men were now busy settling into their new surroundings.

He spotted Russ coming down the pathway, a perplexed look on his face. "What crawled up your ass?" he asked when Russ reached him. "You look all bent out of shape."

"Aw, nothing," Russ replied, scratching his jaw. "Just that one of the bodies from last night is missing, that's all."

Mason raised an eyebrow. "Really?"

The previous night, he'd gotten his men to drag the dead bodies over to the forest edge. That morning, they'd been piled into the back of a truck and dumped at the top of

Camp Benton's driveway. As an ex-guard, Mason knew all about psychological warfare. It was how every prison gang operated.

Russ had gone out with the crew as well. He wanted to scope out the area before Mason's meeting with Sheriff Rollins later that morning. "It's Chris, the leader, that's disappeared," he told Mason. "You sure you killed him last night?"

Mason shrugged. "Last time I looked, his brains were spilling out of a hole I put in his head. He looked pretty dead to me."

Russ appeared satisfied with this. "Coyotes must have come during the night and dragged him away. Or wolves maybe. I hear there's plenty of them around here."

"Must have." Mason drained his cup. "You find a good spot for me to meet the sheriff? I intend on calling him now."

Russ nodded. "I figure the stretch of road between our two camps is best. We can set up shooters on either side to protect you while you two talk. Seeing as we're holding his friend, I don't think he'll risk doing anything. Still, no point in taking chances." He looked at Mason curiously. "What exactly you plan on talking to him about? You haven't told me yet."

"I'm going to give him the option for his people to leave the camp peacefully. Spare him losing any more men. For that, I'll give him back Ned."

Russ looked doubtful. "I'm not sure he'll go for that. The sheriff's got others to think about besides Ned."

"True, but when I tell him I got sixty armed men ready to storm his camp, it's going to freak people out. Some might chose to run off." Mason tapped the side of his head and grinned. "See? That devious mind of yours is starting to rub off on me."

CHAPTER 21

In the bedroom of a large corner house in Old Fort, Ned Granger dozed fitfully. Cracking one eye open, he turned his head toward the window. From the light streaming in through the curtains, he guessed it must be around 8 a.m. He closed his eye again and tried to get back to sleep. However, the pain from his wounds made that difficult.

The injury to his forearm didn't hurt so bad. The bullet had penetrated deep into the muscle tissue and was still lodged there. It was the two other gunshots that were painful. The round that had gone through his right foot had broken several bones, and though the entrance wound was small, where the bullet exited had created a three-cornered tear over two inches wide. The nerve tissue had been damaged, and he couldn't feel his three middle toes.

It was his shinbone that hurt the most, though. The round had badly chipped it before lodging into the calf tissue. Using a pair of tweezers dipped in surgical alcohol to disinfect it, Tania had managed to extract it. Holding the bullet up to him, she'd looked hurt when Granger's expression remained impassive. What did she expect? She was Mason's girlfriend. It wasn't like he was going to gush with gratitude all over her.

Worse than the physical pain was the loss of his three men, Welby, Macey, and Harper. Granger hadn't witnessed that level of violence since his time as a soldier, and their brutal murders had shaken him badly.

He was sure he would join his comrades soon. He was under no illusions why he was still alive. Russ had recognized him as a leading member of the Benton group, one who'd been prominent in organizing the camp's defenses. From what Russ had alluded to the previous day, he knew he would soon be under pressure to reveal all he knew.

Unable to sleep, Granger reviewed his plan one more time on how he would resist divulging any critical information. That he would be tortured, he was in no doubt, and as an ex-soldier, knew he would eventually break. *Everybody breaks.* That was what had been taught to him in the military. A human being could only endure so much pain.

He wouldn't be tortured by a professional interrogator, however. That meant that perhaps he could devise a strategy to determine what he divulged and what he kept secret. The thing he dearly hoped not to reveal was The Ring, the second line of defense he and his team had almost completed before his capture. As well as providing a fallback position, it had been designed to aggressively repel any attacker.

With cleverly-designed interlocking fields of fire that offered an advancing force few blind spots, an overconfident Mason could easily stumble into a nasty trap. The more he thought about it, the more Granger felt that perhaps he could even aid him in doing exactly that. He smiled to himself grimly. In the last few hours of his life, he would do everything in his power to make that happen.

There was the sound of his door being unlocked. His right hand had been cuffed to a heavy chain wrapped around the bed frame, and he turned awkwardly on his side to see Russ enter the room. He was followed in by Doney, a burly man with a pasty face and thick black hair brushed back in a short quiff.

In Doney's right hand was a mug of coffee, in the other, what appeared to be a couple of granola bars. Granger's eyes immediately fixed on them. He hadn't eaten since breakfast the previous day.

"Morning, Ned," Russ said cheerfully. He gestured to the guard. "As you can see, Doney has brought you breakfast in bed. Don't tell me we don't take good care of our guests here. That right, Doney?"

Doney grunted. He handed the coffee mug to Russ. "Here, take this while I uncuff him."

Russ gestured over to the bedside table. "Leave it over there," he instructed. "That's what a bedstand is for."

Doney glared at him a moment, then crossed the room and placed the mug and granola bars down. Reaching into his pocket, he pulled out a key and uncuffed Granger.

Granger sat up in bed, rubbing his wrist, then picked up the mug and took a sip. It was instant coffee, with creamer and sugar. Normally he took it black, but he wasn't complaining. Placing the mug down, he ripped the wrapper off one of the granola bars and bit off a large chunk.

Russ watched him carefully. "Eat up, Ned. You're going to need all your energy today. In an hour's time, you're going to meet your friend, the sheriff."

Granger stopped chewing and a surprised expression came over his face.

Russ chuckled. "Well, *meet* might be a bit of an exaggeration. Perhaps more of a wave. You won't get within three hundred yards of him."

"What's the purpose of that?"

"A smart guy like you ought to know. It's called *proof of life*."

Granger stared at him. Proof of life meant only one thing. Mason intended on trading him for something. What that was, he had no idea. "What are you up to?" he growled.

"Aw, nothing much. Just Mason thinks he can swap your crinkly old ass in exchange for Camp Benton, that's all."

Granger stared at Russ incredulously. "He's crazy! John will never agree to that."

Russ shrugged. "Mason's argument is that seeing as he's taking the camp one way or the other, why not do it without any more loss of life. Including yours. Personally, I'm not convinced."

"He's dreaming," Granger said. "The camp is too well defended. If you thugs try taking it, you'll get your asses kicked."

"We'll see." Russ winked at him. "Now, a little inside knowledge on how your defenses are set up would certainly help the cause, wouldn't it? If you thought about it hard enough, I bet you could easily figure out a way for us to break in."

A contemptuous look came to Granger's face. "I'm not telling you anything. I'd sooner die before I do that."

Russ remained undaunted by his reply. "The trick on my part will be to make sure you don't die until *after* you give us what we want." He gestured over to the bedstand. "Finish your coffee so Doney can cuff you again. Then rest up. It's going to be a long day. If Rollins doesn't agree to Mason's terms, it's going to be an even longer night."

CHAPTER 22

After breakfast, Camp Eastwood's three recruiters set off on their mission. Loading Pete's Tacoma with enough provisions to last them several days, they headed out of camp and down into the valley.

Pete sat behind the wheel with Ralph riding shotgun. In the back seat, Maya, the designated navigator, studied a large roadmap spread across her knees.

As they drove past the camp perimeter, Ralph poked his head out the window to where Cody and Clete stood by the side of track. They'd just dragged a felled tree back to let them by. "So long, suckers!" he yelled, giving them a sloppy salute. "Don't slack off while we're away!"

When they reached the valley floor, Pete pulled onto the old Highway 2 and headed in the direction of Chatsworth. From there, the trio planned to head south along the southern perimeter of the Cohutta, passing through towns such as New Hope, Ellijay, and Amicalola along the way.

If they hadn't found anyone willing to join them by then, they would drive east and check out the towns of Emma and Juno. After the recent showdown with Chris, the three had agreed with Walter that it would be best to search for survivors south of the camp, rather than north. There was no point running into unwarranted trouble.

"Appreciate you guys volunteering to come with me," Pete said once they were a few miles out of camp, holding onto the steering wheel firmly as the pickup dipped and yawed on the highway's uneven surface.

"Seemed like something fun to do," Ralph replied. Though good with a gun, he knew damn-all about living in the boonies, and it had been an impulse decision on his part to volunteer for the task.

In the back seat, Maya sighed. "Turning you into a hillbilly is proving harder than I thought. No sooner have we settled in here than you want to hit town again."

Ralph stared out the window as they wound their way up the side of the Alaculsy Valley. Down below, the rushing waters of the Conasauga River were in view. "Only one-horse towns around these parts," he said. "Soon as you've driven into them, before you know it, you've driven out the far side again. Nothing too exciting about that."

Maya chuckled. "Ralph, haven't you heard? Times have changed. Even a one-horse boonie town has got the potential for excitement these days."

Pete glanced up at her through the rearview mirror. "I daresay you're right. I'm sure we'll run into something strange before this trip's over."

Ralph buzzed his window up and leaned back in his seat. "Here's to hoping. Last time I ran into something strange, I found Maya. Sure pleased how that turned out."

***

Ten miles south of Chatsworth, Pete exited Highway 411 and steered the Tacoma around a dogleg junction before picking up Route 76. The three had spent two hours searching the area for survivors. They'd taken Route 52 and driven to Fort Mountain State Park, reasoning it was the kind of place people might be drawn to. Their reasoning had been correct, and they'd come across a group of eight camped out by a small lake. The group had greeted them with outright hostility, however, and the trio'd left the area quickly.

"This is all getting way too tribal," Maya said with a frown. "It reminds me of a book I read once about an explorer traveling from one side of Borneo to the other. Every jungle village he passed through had some beef going with the one he'd just left. Absolutely no one was getting on. *Uhh*...ring a bell, anybody?"

"Borneo?" Ralph asked, raising an eyebrow. "Aren't those dudes cannibals?"

"Sure used to be. Maybe they are all over again," Pete said. "Let's hope the next place we show up at, they don't try and eat us."

Maya laughed. "Did either of you hear that old joke about the missionary who gets captured in the jungle?" she asked. "The tribe takes him back to their village and throws him into a pot of water. '*Hey, you can't boil me!* he shouts as they light a fire underneath him. '*I'm a friar!*'"

Skirting around the southernmost tip of the Cohutta, the three headed in the direction of Ellijay. There was a large lake nearby. Hopefully they'd find people on their own there, or in pairs. Then it would be up to Pete and Maya to sell them on the great community they were building in the Alaculsy Valley.

At an area called Tails Creek, Maya got Pete to slow down.

"What's up?" he asked.

"According to the map, there's a cluster of lakes and streams behind the forest to our left. Could be worth a look. What do you think?"

Pete came to a halt and Maya passed him the map. Studying it a few moments, he handed it back to her. "Why not? There's a junction a couple of miles ahead. It'll take us up to one of the lakes. Let's see if we get a better reception there than we got at Fort Mountain."

A few minutes later, Pete took an unpaved road into some thinly-forested woodland. On their right, they soon passed a private road that led up to a large house on top of a hill, then around the next bend, a lake came into view.

Pete slowed down. A few hundred yards ahead, two vehicles were parked along the side of the road, one in front of the other. Fifty feet away, a tent had been pitched by the lakeside.

Two men stood by it. One was short and stocky and wore a dark T-shirt, khaki shorts, and hiking boots. The second was taller. He wore a checked shirt and jeans. Both stared at the approaching Tacoma.

"Only two people. This looks more promising," Pete remarked.

"Pull up," Ralph told him. "Let's not get too close until we figure this out."

Pete stopped the pickup in the middle of the road, leaving the engine running. He peered out the windscreen alongside Ralph, assessing the situation.

The nearest vehicle was a silver Volvo. A face suddenly popped up to stare out the back window, and began waving a hand frantically at them.

The men strode over to the car, covering the ground quickly. The taller of the two opened the Volvo's back door and leaned his head in, and whoever was waving stopped. The shorter man stared back at the Tacoma, gesturing aggressively that they should turn around and leave.

Ralph frowned. "I don't like the look of this. Something's up."

"They don't seem like the type we're looking to recruit, that's for sure," Pete said nervously. "Maybe we should just get the hell out of here."

Ralph took his point. In a world where the normal rules of human interaction were dead and buried, a situation like this only invited trouble. Nonetheless, he shook his head. "I don't think we can. The person in the back of that car is a child."

Pete's eyes widened. "You sure? It's too far for me to see properly."

"I'm sure."

Ralph had 20-20 vision. He was in no doubt that the person he'd seen through the back window couldn't have been more than ten years old.

"Given vPox's fatality rate, the chance of either of these two men being their father is slim," Maya said, leaning her head over the seat rests so she could get a better view. "There's no way we can leave here. Not until we find out what's going on. All right, how we going to play this?"

"Turn the car," Ralph told Pete. "Make it look like we're leaving, only park it across the road."

Pete tugged at the wheel and reversed several feet. Putting the car into drive, he drove forward and parked its horizontally across the road.

Ralph grabbed his Bushmaster and opened his door. "Everyone out this side," he ordered, indicating to Pete to follow him out the passenger door.

All three exited, and stood on the far side of the hood facing the two men. The engine block would give them some level of protection from any gunfire that might ensue.

"Hey! What are you doing?" the shorter man yelled warily. Both men had drawn their pistols and had stepped behind the Volvo. "Get the hell out of here!"

"Not before we talk to the kid!" Ralph yelled back, keeping his Bushmaster out of sight below the hood. "Who is that, and what are they doing with you?"

"That's my daughter!" the tall man shouted out. "And she's doing just fine."

"You believe that?" Ralph whispered to Maya.

"Not yet," she whispered back. "Get them to bring her out so we can see for ourselves."

"Bring her out of the car!" Ralph hollered out again. "Soon as we see she's okay, we'll be on our way."

There was the sound of low voices as the two men conferred, then the tall man walked around the side of the vehicle and opened the back door. He leaned in and talked to the person inside.

"There's something very wrong with this," Ralph muttered. "I don't like it one bit."

A moment later, the man stood back and a young girl around eight or nine years old stepped out of the car to stand beside him. She had blonde hair with ringlet curls, and wore a pink T-shirt, shorts, and sandals.

Raising her hand, the girl waved over at the three. "Hi!" she called out in a faltering tone. "I'm okay. Thank you for asking."

"You sure, sweetie?" Maya asked. "You want to come over and talk to us?"

The girl shook her head. "Please…you better go now."

Squinting hard, Ralph stared at the girl's left hand that was nearest to the door. A surge of anger ran through his body. "These two bastards are holding her prisoner," he hissed.

Pete's eyes shot up. "What makes you so sure?"

"Her wrist is tied to something inside the car, probably the door handle. That's why she didn't run out when we got here."

"Sonofabitch," Pete cursed under his breath. "What are we going to do?"

"Soon as she gets back into the car, we're going to take down these sick puppies, that's what. Pete, on my command, you go left, I go right. Got it?"

"Got it."

Maya waved to the girl. "All right, sweetie. You can get back inside now. Bye!"

"Okay…bye!" With a wave of her hand, the girl stepped back into the vehicle.

As soon as the tall man slammed the door shut, Ralph raised the Bushmaster to his shoulder. Taking quick aim, he pulled back on the trigger at short intervals.

Crack! Crack! Crack!

The man doubled over as the first bullet caught him in the stomach. The second and third caught him in the chest and he fell to the ground.

"Go, Pete!" Ralph roared.

Stepping out around the front of the Taco, Ralph sprinted to his right, opening up a field of fire at the remaining man, who'd ducked behind the Volvo again. As he ran, Ralph fired off several more shots, careful to ensure none of them went near the back seat of the vehicle. Glancing to his left, he saw Pete dart behind a tree. He held his pistol in a two-handed grip and began shooting too.

"Stop!" the man yelled in a frightened voice, cowering behind the hood. "I'm not going to shoot."

"Throw your gun out!" Ralph shouted. "Somewhere I can see it."

A moment later, a dark object sailed through the air. It landed in the grass several feet away from the vehicle. Ralph nodded to Pete and the two men strode warily over to him from either side.

Crouched on his heels, the man stared up at Ralph. "Please, don't kill me," he whimpered.

"Get up," Ralph growled.

Maya sprinted over to them. Reaching the Volvo, she pulled open the back door. After peering inside a moment, she turned to Ralph grimly. "Quick, give me your knife."

Ralph unsheathed the tactical knife at his waist and handed it to her. Leaning inside the vehicle, Maya's elbow moved up and down, cutting something.

She stepped back. "All right, sweetie, out you get."

The little girl stepped out of the car. To Ralph's amazement, a moment later, the slender figure of another girl clambered out to stand unsteadily beside Maya.

Perhaps sixteen or seventeen, she had shoulder-length brown hair and wore capris, a short-sleeved cotton blouse, and hiking boots. Both her legs and arms were bound, the reason for her awkward movements. Maya swiftly cut the nylon cord from her wrists. Squatting, she cut the rope binding her feet.

Ralph jabbed the muzzle of the Bushmaster into the man's chest so hard the man cried out in pain. "You sick bastard! Did you hurt these girls?"

"No, I swear to you. We...we only just found them."

"Is that true?" Ralph asked the older girl.

She nodded. "We're okay. Only because you got here in time." Her lower lip quavered. "They planned on taking me into the tent. Said they'd hurt Laura if I put up a fight." She looked over at the younger girl. "She...she doesn't really understand what's going on."

Ralph faced the man again, a dark rage building inside him. "So help me God, I'm going to send you to hell!" he thundered.

"Wait!" Maya cried out. "Let me take the girls away first." Putting her arms around both their shoulders, she led the two girls back to the truck.

"Please...don't," the man said beseechingly. "I swear to you, we were never going to harm her...only...only..."

"Enough," Ralph spat. He prodded the man with the Bushmaster, then gestured for him to walk around to the far side of the Volvo where they wouldn't be seen.

"Give me the Sig," he said to Pete walking beside him, who still held his P226 in his grip.

Pete shook his head. "Can't have you doing all the dirty work," he replied, grim-faced.

Ralph looked at him. "You sure?"

Pete nodded.

Ralph took a couple of steps back while Pete lifted his pistol, placing it against the man's temple. With a whimper, the man closed his eyes.

A shot rang out and he slumped to the ground. Standing over him, Pete put one more round in his head then holstered his weapon. In silence, he and Ralph headed back to their vehicle.

CHAPTER 23

The younger girl, Laura, was nine years old. The older one was seventeen-year-old Jenny. Both sat with Maya in the back of the truck while Pete steered it back toward the highway.

"Where are you girls from?" Maya asked after she had introduced everyone.

"Athens," Jenny replied, untying the remains of the rope from one of her wrists and throwing it out the window. She was the more subdued of the two. Being older, she was aware exactly how dangerous their predicament had been, and it appeared she'd shielded Laura from the reality of the situation.

"Did you know each other before the pandemic?"

Laura bobbed her head vigorously. "We lived in the same apartment block but we weren't really friends. After my mommy and daddy died, Jenny came over to help me."

"I heard her crying when I passed by her door," Jenny explained. "So I brought her back to my apartment. We've been together ever since."

Laura smiled at her serenely. "I'm so lucky you found me."

With her pale skin, bright blue eyes, and golden curls, Ralph couldn't help think just how like a little doll she looked. "How long ago did you leave Athens?" he asked.

"Yesterday. When our food ran out," Jenny replied. "There was no choice."

"We got *so* hungry!" Laura piped up again. "We just had to leave."

Jenny stared at Ralph, holding the Bushmaster between his knees in the front seat, both hands on the barrel. "I can't believe you found us. When you first got out of the car...I...I thought you were Bob and Joe's friends."

Ralph turned sideways in his seat to stare back at her. "Why's that?" he asked.

"Well, because, you...you..."

"Because you look so mean and ugly," Laura interjected. She poked her head through the front seats and frowned. "Are those real scars or is that special effects? You know, like in the movies."

"They're real, little doll. Sorry, I can't just peel them off."

Laura stared at him intently a moment longer. "Cool." She tilted her head back again and faced Maya. "Bob and Joe were *bad*. They tied Jenny up, then they tied me up too. They said if I tried to run off, they would hurt her."

"Bob and Joe aren't going to be bad no more," Ralph grunted.

"I'm glad!" Jenny blurted out. "If you'd let them go, they would have gone off and found some other girls, I'm sure of it."

Maya stared at her with a look of real concern. "Jenny, you sure you're all right? They didn't...you know?"

Jenny shook her head. "They only caught us a little while ago. They'd just finished putting up the tent when you got there."

"Where did they find you?"

"In a town called Dawsonville. We were in a supermarket looking for food. At first they were nice to us, but when we didn't want to go with them, they grabbed us and took us up to the lake. They said if I let them do what they wanted with me, they wouldn't harm Laura. I couldn't have them hurting her, so I agreed. I-I didn't know what else to do. It was awful." Jenny broke off into a sob. Her shoulders shook, and the tears that had been threatening to come all this time poured down her face.

Maya put a hand gently on her shoulder. "It's all right, precious. You're safe now." Other than the sound of Jenny's sobbing, all was quiet in the car.

"Where are we going?" Laura finally asked. "Are you taking us back to your house?"

They had reached the junction of the highway. Pete turned left and headed in the direction of Ellijay. "Not yet," he said, looking up at Laura through the rearview mirror. "We're looking for recruits to take back to our camp. When we've got enough, we'll head back there."

Laura's brow furrowed. "What's a recruit?"

"You know, fellow survivors who want to join our group. Good people we feel will contribute to the camp."

"Cool!" Laura chirped. "Can we be your recruits? We'd like that, wouldn't we, Jenny?"

Jenny wiped the tears from her face and smiled. "Yeah, that'd be great."

Pete glanced over at Ralph and winked. "What you think, partner. You cool with that?"

Ralph pretended to consider things a moment. "Well, Walter didn't exactly say what sort of recruits he was looking for, now did he? Only that they should get along with everybody. Laura and Jenny fit the bill, so yeah, I'm cool with that." He turned in his seat and grinned at the two. "Congratulations, girls. You are officially Camp Eastwood's very first recruits. We're thrilled to have you on board."

CHAPTER 24

Leaving Camp Benton's main checkpoint, Papa Three behind him, Rollins strode down the driveway toward the Cookson Road junction. He was alone, armed with only his police-issue Smith & Wesson concealed in a shoulder holster beneath his jacket.

He was tense. Tired too. Since his early morning conversation with Mason, he hadn't been back to sleep. As soon as their talk ended, he'd doubled the guards along the camp's perimeter, then convened an emergency council meeting.

A short time after that, Liz, the only survivor from the attack on the lodge, arrived at the camp. He and Mary Sadowski talked to her for over an hour, trying to get a sense of how well-armed Mason and his gang were. They gleaned little from the distraught woman other than there had been a least a dozen men, all carrying rifles.

An hour ago, Mason had been back in contact with him. The two agreed to meet on Cookson Creek Road at the midpoint between the two camps. Immediately, Mary had prepared for the meeting, positioning her best marksmen in the trees behind the road. Farther south, they'd seen Mason's men making similar preparations.

Reporting back, Mary informed Rollins that three bodies had been dumped at the top of their driveway. She recognized them immediately as members of the Camp Knox group. Rollins had been shocked. Things didn't bode well for Ned Granger, and he shuddered to think how his friend might be being treated.

Mary had been concerned about the meeting. "John, this could be a trap," she warned him. "You have to wait for Mason to get within shooting range of the snipers before you show yourself. After the meet, you make sure you leave first, you hear? This sonofabitch is hellbent on taking out as many of us as he can before attacking our camp."

Reaching the end of the driveway, Rollins peered around the junction in the direction of the lodge. It was 11:55 a.m. In five minutes, he would meet the killer of three of his men. One who still held his friend Ned Granger captive.

At 12:02 p.m., a black pickup truck emerged around the next bend and came to a stop. Rollins took out a pair of compact binoculars from his jacket pocket and raised them to his eyes. Five hundred yards away, the driver's door swung open and a huge bald man wearing digital camo pants, black boots, and a gray T-shirt stepped out.

He stooped over and talked into the vehicle briefly, then slammed the door and started up the road toward Rollins. Remembering Sadowski's instructions, Rollins waited until he passed a blue ribbon she'd tied to tree as a marker before stepping out onto the road and walking toward him.

When the two men came to within twenty feet of each other, the man stopped and placed his hands on his hips.

"Morning, Sheriff," he said in a distinct low-toned voice that Rollins immediately recognized from their previous conversations. "Glad to see you could make it."

"Before we go any further, you need to show me Ned," Rollins replied tersely, "or this conversation is over before it even begins."

If Mason couldn't prove Granger was still alive, Rollins intended killing him on the spot there and then. He'd take his chances on making it back to safety afterward.

Mason leered at him. "The suspicious type, huh? Well, guess I'd be the same in your situation."

Turning around, he waved his arm. Moments later, from around the back of the pickup, two men dragged a figure out. Rollins pulled out his glasses again to see a haggard but very much alive Ned Granger step into view. His clothes were rumpled and mud-stained, and he had a white bandage around his right forearm. The bottom part of his left jean leg had been cut off, and there was a second bandage wrapped around his shin.

"As you can see, we've been taking care of Ned. My girl patched him up real good."

"You killed three of my men in cold blood, now you're holding my friend prisoner," Rollins said. "You expect me to thank you?"

Mason shrugged. "I got sixty men to take care of. I do what I have to do."

Rollins held his gaze. "I got a lot of people to take care of too, but I don't go around murdering people. All right, Mason, what's this all about?"

"It's pretty simple, Sheriff. You got something I want. Thought you might want to trade it for Ned."

Rollins hesitated. He was sure the terms for saving his friend would be high. He couldn't afford to sound overly keen. "Depends on what you want. I got other folk to consider here, not just Ned. There's only so much in the way of supplies I can give you."

"Nah, I got enough food and ammo to last me a while," Mason responded. "That's not what I'm looking for."

"What then, medical supplies? I could spare a little, I guess."

"Got them too." Mason looked past Rollins and pointed toward the camp driveway. "I hear you got a real nice spread up there by the lake. Good facilities, plenty of cabins.

Perfect place for a group my size. Like I told you, I got over sixty people to take care of."

Rollins stared at him disbelievingly. "You want me to trade our entire camp for Ned?"

"I'm taking it one way or another. Thought you might want to spare any more bloodshed." Mason eyed Rollins up and down. "So…what do you say?"

"You're crazy," Rollins replied, barely keeping his temper under control. "There's no way I can agree to that."

Mason shrugged. "There's probably other people you need to speak to for a decision like that. Go talk to them." He stared back at his pickup. "Radio me by five this evening, otherwise it's not looking good for your friend."

For a brief moment, Rollins was tempted to whip out his M&P9 and plant a bullet in Mason's forehead. Only the vague hope that there might be some way to save Granger held him back. "I'll do that. You'll hear from me soon."

Before Mason could respond, Rollins turned and walked briskly back toward the junction again, just like Mary Sadowski had told him to.

"You got until five o'clock, Sheriff, then Ned's dead!" Mason's deep voice bellowed out after him. "Soon after that, so are you!"

***

"He wants us to do *what*?" Bert Olvan exclaimed, both eyebrows shooting up. "He must be out of his goddamned mind!"

Immediately after returning to camp, Rollins and his three deputies had gone straight to the staff room to discuss what had transpired during his encounter with Mason.

"He's trying to keep us off balance," Rollins replied. "Told me he had sixty men. Maybe I'd have believed him if he hadn't said it twice."

"You sure he's lying?" Henry Perter asked nervously. "We don't stand a chance against that many."

"I can't say for sure. Let's hope Kit has some news when he gets back."

Before the meeting, Rollins had sent one of his men on a scouting mission to Wasson Lodge to assess Mason's strength and, with a bit of luck, find out where he was holding Granger. It seemed an ideal time to do it while everyone was preparing for the encounter on Cookson Creek Road.

Though it was dangerous, Kit Halpern, a young man in his twenties, had immediately volunteered for the assignment. He had been close to the three murdered men, and was determined to do whatever he could to avenge their deaths.

"Then what?" Mary Sadowski asked grimly. "You got a plan to turn this thing around?"

Rollins paused a moment to think, aware that all eyes were on him. The situation between the two groups had quickly turned into a cat and mouse game. Instinct told him it was up to the Bentons to make the next move.

"Soon as we get a better idea of Mason's numbers, we go on the offensive and catch him off guard. It's our best shot at saving Ned. The camp too."

CHAPTER 25

Making as little noise as possible, Kit Halpern paddled out of the main lake and steered his one-man kayak into a narrow inlet no more than thirty feet wide. After a few more strokes, he lifted the two-piece paddle and glided toward where a stand of pines marked the end of the channel. Five hundred yards due south of his position lay Wasson Lodge.

The bank was too steep to drag the kayak out onto. He grabbed a short length of cord attached to the stern's grab handle and tied up to an overhanging branch. Placing his hands to either side of the cockpit, he pulled himself out and clambered up onto the rocks.

Armed with a nine millimeter pistol and a tactical knife, Kit knew just how dangerous the mission he'd volunteered for was. Mason and his bandits had murdered three innocent men and taken Ned Granger hostage. Since then, they'd occupied the lodge, killing most of its occupants.

The loss of his friends at the ambush had been a huge shock. Over the course of the past ten days, Kit had come to know them well. Granger was an experienced soldier, tough but fair. He'd learned a lot from him, also from Bob Harper and Joe Macey. Not only how to fire a weapon, but how to be strong—*inside*, where it really counted. Bob Harper in particular had taken him under his wing and coached him daily, stressing how even though he was still young, he had to remain brave and steadfast in these perilous times. Humanity was counting on it.

Though he burned with anger over their senseless deaths, he knew he had to remain calm and focused if he hoped to help Granger. And Sheriff Rollins's parting words rung in his ears.

"Kit, your first objective is to assess Mason's strength. We need to know how many men he has. Mary will do a head count on Cookson Road, you try and gauge how many men he's left at the camp. If Ned's still alive, Mason will bring him to the meeting to show proof of life. Afterward, when he brings him back to the lodge, see if you can find out where they're keeping him."

Rollins had then placed a hand on his shoulder, staring at him intently. "The most important thing is that you minimize risk. No point in finding out everything only to get yourself killed, you hear?"

Kit set off into the forest. Keeping away from the foot trails, he worked his way through the trees. After two hundred yards, he slowed down. He'd been told that tripwire had been lain around the lodge, and he needed to be careful. Every step he took, he lifted his boot off the ground before placing it slowly down in front of him again.

Ten minutes later, he reached the edge of the forest. Ahead, he could make out the lodge. Outside, a man sat slouched on a stool smoking a cigarette, a semi-automatic rifle leaning against a stack of sandbags next to him.

In front of the building, several pickup trucks were parked in the forecourt while behind, facing out onto the lake, was a large open field. In the middle were four trailers in a neat row. Scattered untidily around them were several more RVs—an assortment of camper vans, Winnebagos, and travel trailers, in front of which people either stood chatting or sat at tables, drinking from coffee mugs.

Kit squatted behind a large tree and took out a notebook and pen. He began the head count, also sketching out the defensive configuration of the camp. Over the course of the next fifteen minutes, he added to the count as several other men, and a few women, came in and out of the trailers. In total, he counted eleven men and four women.

He had to wait a while longer before he heard the sound of engines. Moments later, a black GMC Canyon appeared on the driveway, followed by a bottle-green Ford F-150. Tailing them was a big-engined motorcycle of some description.

All three vehicles pulled up directly in front of the lodge. The door to the GMC opened and an enormous bald-headed man got out. Simultaneously, four armed men jumped out of the load bed. Or, at least three of them were armed. Squinting, Kit recognized the last one to gingerly haul himself down off the tailgate as Ned Granger.

His breath quickened as the group headed in his direction, toward where the guard now stood attentively at his post. Kit pressed his body close against the tree, not daring to stick as much as his nose out.

As they got closer, he could hear them perfectly. "Russ, you need to get to work on Ned," a deep-toned voice spoke out. "I need information before we hit their camp tonight."

"Tonight?" A higher-pitched voice replied in a surprised tone. "You plan on taking the camp that soon?"

"Nah, we'll just do a hit and run, shake them up some more. Just see to it that Ned helps us out. You can do that for us, can't you, Ned?"

"Go to hell, Mason. You won't get anything from me, you sonofabitch!" the defiant voice of Ned Granger retorted.

There was a chuckle before Mason spoke again. "Guess you're going to need that blowtorch after all, Russ. Told you."

The second man laughed. "Not sure if I can find one that easy. Don't worry, I got everything I need to make him talk."

"Good," Mason grunted. "Grab some lunch, then take him back to Old Fort where no one can hear him scream. I don't want Tania complaining about it. Women are kinda squeamish about that sort of thing."

There was some more laughter, then the voices receded as they headed farther into the field.

Kit crept back from the tree and stole away into the forest. His job was done. Now all he had to do was make it back to his canoe without setting off the tripwire. He had plenty of information for Rollins. He couldn't risk blowing things now.

CHAPTER 26

At Zephyr House, its four inhabitants got started on the garden. Reminding Fred that she was the only *real* farmer among them, Marcie made the decision on what vegetables they should plant.

After breakfast, she rummaged through a large supermarket bag, the one Fred had filled up in a gardening store in Maysville. She pulled out several seed bags and placed them on the kitchen table.

"What you got there?" Fred asked suspiciously. "Remember, it's June. Not everything is going to germinate in this heat."

Marcie grabbed the seed bags and tossed them onto his lap. "Take a look for yourself," she said curtly.

Simone struggled to contain a smile. She couldn't help but think how similar in nature Fred and Marcie were, like two cantankerous twins that had been separated at birth.

Fred sifted through the bags. "Carrots... broccoli... beetroot... turnips. Hmph, I suppose they'll do." He looked across the table at Eric. "Come on, Eric, take me to the garden."

The garden wasn't a garden at all, but the large field to the side of the house in which Simone and Marcie had originally spotted Eric. About half an acre in size, it was covered in lush green grass, and had an apple orchard in one corner.

"I'd prefer to work at the back of the house where we can stay out of sight," Fred explained while Eric wheeled him down a narrow, rutted path that ran along one side of the field, "but I don't think the land is good enough."

"It isn't. I checked it out this morning," Marcie agreed, walking behind Eric. "It's too steep, and the bottom is one big swamp. No good for growing anything; not without a lot of hard work."

Getting Eric to stop halfway down the path, Fred pointed toward the middle of the field where the ground was slightly elevated. "Right about there. That's where we should dig our beds. Someplace they'll get plenty of sun."

"No." Marcie pointed over to the far corner of the field. "We'll dig the beds over there," she said firmly. "They'll still get plenty of sun, but with less wind. The shrubbery line and that stand of apple trees will protect them."

"It's thick with weeds there," Fred protested. "I can see them from here. That'll only make our job harder."

"And why do you think those weeds are over there and not your patch?" Marcie retorted. "Good soil and good drainage, that's why." Spade in hand, she set off across the field before Fred could reply.

Grinning, Simone exchanged glances with Eric, forgetting for a moment he was blind.

Perhaps reading her mind, he broke out into a smile too. "Now, Fred. Stop jumping down Marcie's throat. Maybe that way, she won't jump down yours either."

"She jumps down mine a lot farther than I can ever go," Fred grumbled disconsolately. "All right, eighty degrees right and full ahead!" he yelled. "Chop, chop, Eric, get after her. Don't make me have to use the whip!"

All three laughing, Eric turned the wheelchair hard right and pushed it off the footpath and into the field. Carrying a large canvas bag full of gardening equipment, Simone ran after them.

By the time they reached her, Marcie had already dug a large divot in the ground. Bent over, she inspected the topsoil, deeming it to be of decent quality. After further inspection, she declared the drainage to be good as well. With Simone's help, the two marked out the designated digging area with wooden stakes and twine.

The team formed into a production line. Perhaps not the most efficient one in the world, but one that kept the four busy, and gave them all a sense of satisfaction that they were contributing to the effort.

At the top of the line, Eric led off, turning the earth with the spade Marcie handed him. Simone came next, using a garden fork to break up the rich black soil, picking out weeds and thistles and chucking them to one side. Next came Marcie, who carefully planted the seeds into the tilled earth. Last, but not least, Fred bellowed out instructions, keeping Eric in a straight line and pointing out any weeds Simone might have missed.

"Just as well I'm half deaf," Marcie grumbled to Simone, five yards in front of her, as Fred barked out yet another command in his harsh guttural voice. "Otherwise I'd have tipped his damned chair over by now."

When they completed the first row, Marcie looked back along the seed bed with satisfaction. "Not bad. I don't think we'll win any awards in *Fine Gardening*, but we're getting there." She looked over at Fred. "All right, Sergeant Major. Get the troops back in line, I want these carrots planted by lunchtime."

***

At 1 p.m., they went back to the house and ate a lunch of pasta, tinned tuna, and pickled beetroot. Afterward, Marcie stood up from the table and made coffee.

Grabbing a pot, she went over to the sink and filled it from the hot water tap. None of them had any idea how much was still left up in the water tank. Back at her farmhouse in Clemson, Marcie had had an eighty-gallon tank. She knew that because she and Dan had recently taken out the old galvanized tank from the attic, replacing it with a larger, more efficient one that served both the cold and hot water systems.

She took the pot over to the island and lit a ring on the tiny camping stove Fred and Eric had brought with them. "Fred, how do you feel about lending me and Simone your station wagon for a couple of hours?" she asked, dumping several spoonfuls of coffee from the mason jar into the pot.

Over by the table, Fred gazed at her suspiciously. "What the hell for?"

"I want to see if any farm animals have survived in the area. If we find any, no reason why we can't hitch a trailer and bring them back here. In fact, if we find an unoccupied farm with good facilities, maybe we ought to consider moving to it."

"I'm not moving anywhere. I like it here," Fred said firmly. "But if you want to go rescue some animals, knock yourself out." He gestured over to one of the cabinets by the far wall. "Keys are in the drawer. Just take it easy with her, she's old. Used to belong to my next door neighbor."

"Don't worry," Marcie assured him. "I had an old station wagon that me and Dan had forever. Always treated it real good. Broke my heart to leave it on the highway yesterday." She cracked a smile. "But every cloud has a silver lining, they say. If I was still riding around in my own vehicle, most likely I wouldn't be here right now."

"Right," said Fred dryly. "And that would be just the darnedest shame."

CHAPTER 27

At the corner house in Old Fort, the afternoon sun beat down hard on the living room window. Without air conditioning, it was hot and stuffy inside, and a trickle of sweat ran down the side of Ned Granger's face. However, the insufferable heat was the least of his problems.

He sat on a high-backed kitchen stool in the center of the room. Stripped to the waist, his hands were bound tightly behind his back, both ankles tied to the legs of the stool. One of his guards was sprawled on the living room sofa, while the other stood by the window browsing a glossy magazine.

Russ stood in front of Granger. "Seriously, Ned, I don't want to do this," he said, opening up the conversation. "You know what I'm talking about, don't you? The blood, the broken bones, the terrifying screams. To be honest, I'm squeamish about that kind of stuff."

"Sounds like Mason gave you a bum deal," Granger replied. "If it makes you feel better, we can swap places. I don't mind."

Russ chuckled. "Why Ned, you got a sense of humor after all. Don't think I noticed it before. All right, down to business. Like Mason told you, we need information on Camp Benton's perimeter defenses. How about we start off with how many guards will be posted tonight, and where they'll be placed. After that, we'll move onto where you think is the best point for us to attack."

Granger snorted. "You're out of your mind if you think I'm going to tell you that."

"Why does something tell me it's *you* that's going to be out of your mind pretty soon?" Russ paused a moment. "I wasn't kidding about being squeamish. Bearing that in mind, I thought we might go about this interrogation in a less violent manner."

He walked across to the far side of the room and picked up a plastic watering can and a large piece cloth, holding them up for Granger to see. "You have any idea how easily these two household items can be used to extract information from a person?"

Granger stared at him, frozen faced. He knew exactly how effective the form of torture Russ referred to was. It had been used for centuries all over the world. Long before 9/11, US soldiers in Vietnam had used it to extract information from the Viet Cong, and vice versa.

"It's called waterboarding," Russ continued, walking back over to him. "Funny thing is, back when I first read about it during the whole Gitmo thing, it fascinated me. So I spent time researching it on the Internet. You know, the way you do."

"The way sick puppies do, you mean."

Russ chuckled. "I'll take that as a compliment. Point is, never in my wildest dreams did I ever think I'd get the opportunity to waterboard somebody myself one day. Yet look at me, look at you, in a world gone to hell. Funny isn't it?"

"Hilarious," Granger replied.

"Did you know Sheik Mohammed, al Qaida's 9/11 mastermind, lasted only two minutes when the CIA used this technique on him? Bawled like a baby, begging to tell them everything." Russ stared at Granger. "It'll be interesting to see if you cry like a baby. You don't seem the type. Then again, neither did the sheik."

Granger stared at him contemptuously. "You wouldn't last ten seconds. If you were in my shoes, you'd already have wet your pants by now."

Russ leered at him. "Unfortunately for you, that's never going to happen, is it?" He waved over to the guards. "If my two assistants could join me please?"

The two guards stared at each other, annoyed frowns on their faces. They came over to stand on either side of Granger.

"Tip his chair all the way back," Russ ordered them. "Slowly now."

The men gripped Granger by each shoulder and lowered him to the floor while Russ walked over to the sofa and grabbed a couple of cushions. He brought them back and placed one under each stool leg so that Granger's head tilted back at an angle. "Works best this way, if I remember right."

Everything went dark when Russ placed the cloth over Granger's forehead so that it covered his eyes, nose, and mouth. Somebody held the other side of it firmly while another pressed down on his chest. A moment later, water ran over his face and rushed up inside his nostrils.

He held his breath for as long as he could, leading to a feeling of being smothered. Finally, he was forced to breathe, and immediately sucked water into his lungs. A feeling of terror enveloped him and he felt himself drowning. Desperate, he tried to expel the water, but was forced to inhale even more.

On his next breath, he started gagging when food material traveled up his esophagus. It was how many victims of waterboarding died—from aspiration of their own vomitus.

The cloth was removed and the hands holding him lifted off him. Coughing and spluttering, Granger leaned over and heaved up water and vomit onto the floor.

"Holy shit!" Russ exclaimed.

Seconds later, before he'd even had a chance to recover, Russ nodded to the guards and the two men pushed

Granger down again. "All right, Ned. Ready for round two? Ding, ding!"

"Stop, I'll tell you everything!" Granger cried out hoarsely. His mind raced, trying to remember exactly what he planned on divulging to Russ. "Just don't—"

Russ grinned wickedly. "Sorry, but they say you should do the procedure at least twice if you want to get the *real* truth from a person. Besides, I need to see this one more time."

Granger had just enough time to collect a deep breath before the room went dark again. The next moment, the water poured over his face. Soon his lungs would burst, and he would be forced to inhale it once more. His entire body shuddered.

Behind him, there was the sound of footsteps in the hallway. Granger heard the door slam open, and immediately the hands that held him down lifted.

"What the hell!" Russ cried out.

Several pistol shots rang out in quick succession. Lying on his back, Granger shook his head vigorously from side to side until the cloth slid off his face. Sucking in a mouthful of air, wild-eyed, he looked around the room.

To either side of him, the two guards lay motionless on the floor. Standing next to them, an open-mouthed Russ held both hands in the air. "Please…don't shoot," he whimpered.

Granger turned his head to see the lanky figures of Henry Perter, Kit Halpern, John Rollins, and two other men step into the room.

"Ned, you all right?" Perter asked, rushing over to him. He knelt beside him and, with a knife, began to slice off the nylon ropes that bound him to the chair.

"I'm fine. Never happier to see you, old friend."

Perter stared down at him, relief flooding his face. He grinned. "I believe that's what they call 'just in the nick of time.'" Offering a hand, he lifted Granger to his feet.

Granger turned to face Russ, who wore a look of complete

shock. "What was that you said about how you would never be in my shoes?" he asked. He leaned over and picked up the watering can. "Come on, Hank, let's go. I want to see how many seconds it takes for this weasel to bawl like a baby. Not long, I suspect."

CHAPTER 28

By now, Billy had become used to his solitary existence. Most days passed by fine, so long as he didn't dwell on things too much, especially the day he dragged his parents up to the ditch and set them alight. God, how he wished he hadn't turned around that one last time to gaze down at his mother's ravaged face as her hair crackled in the flames. It was an image etched indelibly in his mind.

It was nighttime, though, that brought the terrors, when his defenseless mind became besieged by nightmares and he would wake up from his own screaming, covered in a thick film of sweat. Often, he would sleep under his bed, his shotgun beside him, until the first tendrils of a new dawn crept in through his window. Sometimes it was the only way he could deal with things, and stop himself getting spooked by the loneliness of it all.

**

After lunch, Billy strolled up the garden path and made his way through the fruit bushes to where the chicken tractor sat parked in the shade of an apple tree. It was built out of old pallets, plywood, and chicken wire. In it were three roosters and fifteen hens. There were Welsummers, Orpingtons, and

Plymouth Rocks that between them laid beautiful brown, pink, and speckled eggs.

He unlatched the mesh panel door and stepped inside. After several efforts, he managed to grab a twelve-week-old Orpington, a breed his father liked to select for eating. Although there was still some meat left in the pantry, it was better he kept what remained for emergencies. Today he would take the step that he'd always known he would have to take.

Although he had never slaughtered an animal before, he'd watched his father do it many times. His father felt that Billy should be exposed to the realities of life at an early age, and a few days after his tenth birthday, he'd brought him into the shed where the farm's livestock was butchered.

"People have become too removed from the food chain," his father told him as he expertly killed and gutted a rabbit for dinner that evening. "It's led to disgraceful practices at factory farms where the animals are treated terribly. Here at Willow Spring, we raise and slaughter our livestock humanely, and know that the meat we put on the table is clean and healthy."

Today, Billy wouldn't kill a rabbit. A rabbit displayed fear far too similar to that of a human for him to bear. Watching his father chop a chicken's head off, however, didn't affect him nearly as much. Besides, roast chicken was his favorite dinner.

Locking the tractor door, he wrapped his arm tightly around the chicken and strode across the garden to the butchering shed. Inside, the water he'd put on earlier was coming to a boil, and he switched the propane burner off.

He grabbed a plastic feed bag and put the chicken inside it, thrusting its head out through a hole cut in one corner. That way, it was easier to hold the bird still, and it wouldn't flop around and bruise the meat while he killed it.

He took it over to the corner of the shed where a tree stump, which served as the chopping block, sat on the floor. Lying the bird's head down on it, he picked up the axe resting against the stump and mumbled a few words. Words he was never entirely sure what his father meant by. Something about asking forgiveness for taking the animal's life, and that its body would go to good use.

It was part of an ancient Cherokee ritual. The Cherokee were woodland Indians who'd controlled vast territories of Georgia, Tennessee, and the Carolinas. They'd hunted a variety of different animals: deer, fox, rabbit, turkey, even bear, his father had told him, and respected nature, using every part of an animal's body after they killed it. At Willow Spring Farm, Billy's father had liked to do the same.

Holding the chicken firmly with his left hand, Billy raised the axe. The axe head was sharp. With one deft stroke, he severed the bird's head, then dropped the axe to the floor. Grabbing the bird firmly with both hands, he held onto it until its reflexes finally stopped. He let go and breathed a sigh of relief. That had gone better than he'd expected.

He pulled the chicken out of the bag by its legs, walked over to the pot, and dropped it into the scalding water, dunking it several times before testing a couple of feathers. After the fifth dunk, they slid out without resistance.

He strung the bird up from a nylon cord that hung from one of the rafters. Placing a metal bucket underneath it, he began the process of plucking it. The feathers all came off easily and it took no more than a few minutes. He rinsed off the carcass and placed it back on the block for *evisceration*, as his father called it.

At the joint of the leg, he cut off the feet with a narrow-bladed skinning knife, then cut around the opening of the neck, pulled out the vent—the part where the chicken held its food. Turning the carcass around, he made a larger cut and pulled out the intestines and organs, dropping everything into the bucket.

He wiped his brow. It was done. The chicken was ready for cooking. That evening he would stuff it full of garlic and thyme, and roast it in the oven, just like he'd helped his mother do dozens of times before. Next, he would butcher a rabbit. Billy closed his eyes and tried to imagine that. He shuddered. It would be a lot harder than killing a bird.

He'd just finished washing his hands when he heard the sound of an engine coming down the driveway. Instantly, he froze. Could that be the intruders from the other day returning?

He grabbed the Remington shotgun he'd left by the shed door and slipped out quietly, making his way back through the garden. When he reached the back of the house, he hid behind a tree and peeked around it.

Shading his eyes, he spotted a figure standing by the kitchen window. From this distance, it was too far for him to see properly. He stepped away, quietly skirting around the bramble hedge that bordered the garden, then darted along the sidewall toward the front of the house. When he reached it, he saw an old gray station wagon parked outside. This was a different set of intruders.

He walked over to the entrance to see the front door wide open, its frame torn once more at the latch. A surge of anger ran through him to think that he had been broken into yet again.

He stepped in through the doorway and crept down the hall, his shotgun leveled at his shoulder. When he reached the end, he took a deep breath, pushed the kitchen door open with the muzzle of the Remington and burst in.

"Freeze!" he shouted at a figure wearing dungarees and work boots. He knelt on his haunches with his head in one of the kitchen cabinets.

The figure jerked its head out and stared at him in alarm. To his surprise, Bill saw that it was an old lady with gray hair tied in a bun. She appeared even older than his granny, Esther, who used to visit the farm from West Virginia twice a year.

"Oh my Lord!" she gasped, staring at the shotgun leveled at her head. "Easy with that, child, lest it goes off." Her eyes flicked over to where a similar weapon rested against one of the worktops. "See, I got a gun just like that. They can go off by accident real easy."

Billy jacked a shell into the Remington's chamber, holding the barrel steady. "If this gun goes off, it won't be by accident," he said fiercely. "That's all a thief like you deserves."

The old lady shook her head indignantly. "Hey, I'm no thief! We were passing by and saw the sign for Willow Spring Organics. Thought there might be some farm animals we could rescue. We had no idea someone was living here."

Billy stared at her sharply. "*We?* Who is we?"

"'We' is me and Marcie," another female voice uttered softly behind him. Billy spun around to find himself facing a pretty black girl in her late teens standing by the back door. She wore a leather jacket, sneakers, and jeans. In her outstretched hand, a pistol was pointed at his chest.

"Easy, child," the older woman said behind him. "Put the gun down. That way no one gets hurt."

Billy stared at the girl. Their eyes locked. "Who, me?" both said simultaneously after a moment's hesitation.

The old lady chuckled. "Well now you two have me confused. Tell you what, how about you both put them down?"

There was something about the two women that Billy trusted. Neither talked like the intruders that had come before. "I'll put mine away, if you do the same," he said.

The girl nodded.

Billy lowered his shotgun and rested the butt on the floor. Immediately, the girl dropped her pistol and shoved it inside her jacket pocket. She stepped into the kitchen and the two looked at each other awkwardly.

"I'm Simone, by the way," the girl said.

"I'm Billy."

Simone pointed over to the older woman. "That's my friend Marcie. Sorry, we didn't realize anyone was living here."

"It's okay. So long as you help me fix the door. That's the second time it's been broken down."

Simone smiled apologetically. "Of course." She looked around. "Are you here on your own?"

Billy nodded.

"Your parents?"

"They're both dead."

"Lord, that must have been hard on you, child, left all on your own like this," the old lady said. Though her voice crackled harshly, there was real concern in it.

Without warning, Billy felt his defenses crumble. He'd lost count of how many days he'd been on his own. During that time, he'd dragged his parents into a field and set them alight, he'd looked after the farm and stayed out of the clutches of intruders. Worst of all, the thing he hid from himself in order to survive, was the ice-cold loneliness that buried itself deeper into his heart each day. It all chose that moment to catch up with him.

"Real hard," he croaked. "I was so…*lonely.*" Without being able to help himself, his chest heaved, and his eyes flooded with tears.

Simone came over to him. She put her arms around him and held him close to her. "It's all right, Billy. You're with friends now."

Marcie walked over to both of them and put an arm over each of their shoulders. "That's right. You got me and Simone now. You need never be lonely again."

Billy sniffled, then stepped back and composed himself, embarrassed that he'd broken down like that. "You want I show you the farm?" he asked. "There's fifteen acres of land here. We got our own spring too."

"Wow, that's a lot of land," Simone said. "Did your parents work it by themselves?"

Billy nodded. "Some of it's just forest, though. And I helped too. Most days."

"You got any farm animals here?" Marcie asked.

"Yes, there's chickens, rabbits, and ducks. Also a pig and two goats. I can manage them easily. It's the gardening that's hard."

Marcie exchanged glances with Simone before speaking again. "Billy, remember what we just said about you never needing to be alone again?"

Billy nodded.

"How do you feel about me and Simone coming to stay here and helping you with the work? See if we don't all get along?"

"I-I'd like that," Billy said, blinking hard.

"One thing, though. We have two friends. There's Fred, a man my age who's wheelchair bound, and his friend Eric, who is blind. If we can convince them to come, could they stay here too?"

"That fine. It doesn't sound like they could manage on their own anyway."

Marcie chuckled. "They do better than you might think. I have to warn you, though, Fred's a cranky old goat. We may have to leave him in your barn on occasion. Maybe he can keep your goats company."

***

Fred took the news about the farm surprisingly calmly. Perhaps the solemn figure of Billy Bingham who stood before him in the kitchen had something to do with that. Marcie had wisely left it for Billy to describe to him the merits of moving to an operational farm, and despite his stubborn comment earlier, Fred was quick to admit how much more practical it would be.

"You say you keep chickens and rabbits?" he said, wheeling forward until he was no more than a foot away from the boy. "It's been almost two weeks since I've eaten fresh meat."

"Yes sir. We also got ducks, a pig, and two goats."

"Goats? What do you want them for?" Fred asked, frowning. "Goats eat everything in sight."

"We make milk and cheese from the doe, and use William to pull the field cart."

Fred raised an eyebrow. "You're called Billy, and your billy goat is called William. Have I got that right?"

Billy nodded, a serious look on his face. "I'm named after my grandfather, but that was before we brought the goats to the farm. My father named the billy goat William so neither of us would get confused when he shouted at us. That's what he liked to say. It's a joke. My father never shouted at me. At least, not much."

"Sounds like he was a good man. And had a fine sense of humor too." Fred spun one wheel of his chair to face Marcie. "You played that perfectly, old woman. Nothing like a strong upstanding boy like Billy here to get to my soft side." He spun the wheel back around again. "How big is this farmhouse of yours? Will it fit all five of us?"

"There's only two bedrooms, but the living room is big. It's got two sofas."

Fred considered this. "Me and Eric bed down in the living room here. No reason why we can't do the same at your place." He frowned. "One more thing. How do you feel about Marcie and Simone sleeping in your parents' bedroom. That bother you at all?"

Billy nodded emphatically. "I'd like that. It's been scary upstairs on my own. Sometimes I sleep under the bed."

Fred let out a satisfied grunt. "That's settled then. Tomorrow, we'll all go over and take a look. If the place is as nice as you say, we can spend the day moving our stuff over. Shouldn't take more than a couple of trips."

Simone stole a glance at Marcie, to see a relieved expression on her face. After their tour of Willow Spring, both were in no doubt that it was a far better setup than Zephyr House. Thanks to Billy, their talk with Fred had gone according to plan. Things were progressing smoothly.

CHAPTER 29

Mason Bonner sat at the camping table under the awning of his trailer. He stared out across the lake at the beautiful sunset before him.

The skies were suffused in a rich palette of red, saffron, and pomegranate pink, while shafts of soft golden rays shone down onto the tranquil waters. Though a city dweller his entire life and not normally prone to the wonders of nature, he couldn't help but feel a certain awe. At times like these, he even wondered whether perhaps there might be a Heaven. He prayed not. For if there was a Heaven, then there must be a Hell, and he knew which of the two he would be destined for.

His reverential state quickly dissipated when, from the corner of his eye, he saw Tania come down the steps of the trailer carrying two steaming hot bowls of spaghetti carbonara. She placed one down in front of him, then sat opposite him. Mason stared down at the ungainly heap of stodgy pasta, the sweet, sickly smell of bottled cream sauce wafting under his nostrils.

Pouring a glass of Chianti for them both, Tania started on her dinner. She wound a roll of dripping spaghetti around her fork and shoved it into her mouth with a loud slurp, then picked up her glass and washed the food down her throat.

"What's wrong, babe?" she asked, staring at him over the rim of her glass. "Too hot for you still?"

"Yeah," Mason muttered. "That must be it."

"Drink some wine until it cools down a little," Tania advised, indicating to his untouched glass.

Mason reached forward and grabbed the can of beer beside his crystal goblet and took a long slug. He hated wine. Hated the buzz, hated the hangover even more. Beer, vodka, whiskey, that he could drink all night and still feel fine the next day, chipper even. Wine made him puke.

He checked his watch. It was 4:57 p.m. Rollins was due to call him right about now, though most likely he wouldn't bother, Mason reasoned. After all, what was there to say? He doubted the Benton survivors had any intention of giving up their camp for just one man.

As soon as he finished his meal, he intended calling the sheriff instead. Fuck with him some more. Tell him all the things he intended to do to Ned.

A thought occurred to him. After supper, he'd drive down to Old Fort so Rollins could hear Ned's screams for himself. The idea appealed to him. Smiling, he reached for his knife and fork. Despite the unappetizing dish that sat in front of him, he was hungry. Mason was a big man. He needed to eat regularly to keep up his strength.

He was about to shove a mouthful of pasta down his gullet when his radio crackled to life.

"Mason, do you copy me? This is Sheriff Rollins, over."

Mason leaned forward and grabbed the radio from off the chair beside him. "Read you loud and clear," he replied. "You're a punctual man, Sheriff. So what's the news? You intend saving Ned or not? Over."

There was a slight delay before Rollins's calm voice spoke again. *"As you can imagine, me and my council have been working this thing all day. In the end, we all agreed that Ned's safe return is what matters most to us. Over."*

A surprised grin came over Mason's face. It seemed like Rollins and his people were willing to give up their camp to save their friend after all. He couldn't wait to tell Russ how wrong he was when he returned from Old Fort.

He stood up from the table and stepped away to lean his shoulder against the side of the trailer. "Sheriff, you came to the right decision. Got to admire you for that. No point in any more innocent lives being lost. When do you intend moving out? Soon as I see you're serious about this, I'll release Ned."

A loud chuckle came over the airwaves. *"You misunderstand me. Perhaps I didn't make myself clear. We have no intention of vacating the camp, over."*

"Then what the hell you talking about?" Mason growled. "Don't fuck with me Rollins, or I'll go to work on Ned with a blowtorch. You can listen to him scream over the radio. How about that, you piece of shit?"

There was another chuckle. *"Tell you what, Mason. How about I put you on to a* real *piece of shit? Maybe he can explain things better than me."*

There was a short pause before the radio came back to life. A familiar voice spoke in a quavering tone. A voice Mason had gotten to know well over the past couple of weeks.

"Mason...it's me...Russ. Don't ask me how, but the sheriff tracked us down to Old Fort. He's got Ned back and taken me prisoner."

"What the fu—"

"He's got a proposition for you. Please Mason, do as he says, or else they're going to do terrible things to me..." Russ became practically unintelligible as he broke down. *"Awful things,"* he sobbed. *"You have no idea."*

A moment later, Rollins came back on the radio. *"All right Mason, I'm going to keep this real simple. You got until the day after tomorrow for you and your men to move out of the lodge. After that, like Russ says, we're going to do terrible things to him. Over and out."*

Lowering the handset, Mason stared at it in disbelief while an unrelenting pressure started to build in his head. Slowly at first, then it quickly gathered pace. His cheeks burned and he felt like his eyes were about to pop out of their sockets.

Tania stared at him uncertainly, absently twirling her fork in a mound of spaghetti. "Babe…are you all right?"

A succession of fireworks erupted in Mason's head. "*Yaaaaarghhh!*" he yelled, exploding into an uncontainable fury.

He dropped the radio and stumbled toward the table. Grabbing it by either side with his massive hands, he hurled it into the air. To the sound of Tania's shrieks, the pasta bowls and wine goblets rose into the air. Somersaulting in a three-sixty turn, their contents came crashing down over her head.

She sobbed hysterically as spaghetti strands coated in thick carbonara sauce dripped down her face. "Mason! Why did you *do* that?"

Another savage roar emanated from Mason's belly. "*Waaauuurruughh!*" he bellowed. "Rollins! I'm going to kill you!"

***

In Camp Benton's staff room, a grinning Sheriff Rollins placed the radio back on the table. Despite the trauma of the past twenty four hours, he'd gotten a kick out of being able to turn the tables on Mason. More than anything, he felt a huge relief that he and his men had been successful in rescuing Ned Granger.

When Kit Halpern had returned to camp, excitedly telling him that Granger was being taken somewhere in Old Fort, Rollins had immediately rounded up a team of six men to go find him. Kit had been one of them, determined to seek revenge for his fallen companions.

Driving out of camp, they'd turned right onto Cookson and shot up the road, Rollins praying that Mason didn't spot them, or if he did, that he didn't guess their intentions.

Twenty minutes later, they arrived in Old Fort. After circling the streets endlessly, Kit eventually spotted a bottle-green pickup truck and a Suzuki VStrom parked outside a corner house on a residential back street.

Parking on the next road, the men had made their way to the back of the house and climbed over the garden wall, entering through the unlocked kitchen door. Surprising Granger's three captors in the living room, he and his men had killed two of them. When a terrified Russ immediately thrust his hands in the air, Rollins instructed his men not to kill him.

On arrival back at camp, Granger had insisted he was fine. After washing and changing clothes, he'd gotten straight back to work. This thing was far from over. No way in hell was Mason the kind of person who would just get up and leave Wasson Lodge. And no way in hell did Granger not want to be involved in the plan to oust him.

Bert Olvan and Henry Perter stood to either side of their handcuffed prisoner. "All right guys, lock him up. We're done with him for the moment. Tonight, I'll begin with his interrogation." He leered at Russ. "You know how that goes, don't you?"

"Please, Ned, I-I'll tell you everything. There's no need to hurt me," Russ said in a barely audible voice. "I'm not a brave man. I can't pretend otherwise."

Granger stared at him coldly. "Trouble is, Russ, I don't believe you. I got to dunk you twice to make sure you tell me the truth. That's what you said, right?"

With a whimper, Russ's legs buckled. Olvan and Perter seized him roughly by the arms and dragged him out of the room.

"Ned, you really intend on waterboarding him?" Mary Sadowski asked curiously as soon as Russ had left the room.

Granger shrugged. "Right now, my inclination is yes. I'll see how I feel later."

"Good," Sadowski replied. "After what he did to our three boys, that weasel-faced sonofabitch deserves everything he gets."

"I won't hold you back," Rollins said. Earlier, Granger had gone over everything that had transpired since the ambush. Russ had been involved in everything, including the murders of Chris and his men at the lodge.

"I was just a young man during 9/11," he reflected. "To be honest, I never felt comfortable about our treatment of prisoners at Guantanamo Bay. I felt that as Americans we needed to show the world we had principles. That we had a core decency that couldn't be corrupted. Torture isn't *decent*.

"Then a decade later, ISIS emerged, an even more brutal regime. I was older then, more mature, and my reasoning changed. I figured that although we shouldn't advertise the means by which we got information from our enemies, we had to do whatever it took to protect our country from those who were intent on destroying it. That included torture." Rollins shrugged. "We change as we get older. The more we see, the harder our hearts grow. Just the way it is."

"And now?" Sadowski asked quietly. "Have you changed again since the pandemic? Have you grown even harder?"

Rollins leveled his gaze at her. "Absolutely, Mary. Mankind has just survived an extinction level event. Now we need to make sure the good guys win. By whatever means necessary."

CHAPTER 30

Around 8 p.m., as the last of the summer light dwindled from the skies, the group of five halted for the night. Exiting off US 19, Pete turned onto a minor road and headed for Toto Creek Park, marked by Maya on the map as a potential place to find survivors.

Earlier, when touring the area around Ellijay, they'd encountered a group of twelve people who had taken over a small farm. Though not as hostile as the group at Fort Mountain, they'd made it clear that Pete and his group should move on right away.

It had been over two weeks since the pandemic first swept across the nation, and it appeared that those who'd wanted to join larger groups had done so already. Those traveling alone or in pairs were rare sightings, and the few they'd come across had either run away into the forest or stared at them with crazed expressions. Another two lay dead by the shores of a lake outside an area called Tails Creek.

"The survivor recruitment business…hardest game in the world," Ralph remarked dryly as they pulled into the park. "Glad I'm only the muscle around here. No pressure on me."

Toto Creek Park was a small national park located on the northwest corner of Lake Lanier. The facilities were primitive, no more than a few basic campsites that had never had electricity or potable water.

Driving around, they saw no signs of human habitation. Not a single RV or tent pitched anywhere.

"I guess this is a good a place as any to pull up for the night," Pete said, halting at the third campsite they visited. It had a triangular-shaped lawn with six or seven camping spots spread around it, each with a wooden picnic table beside them.

In the dusk, the place looked a little spooky. "You sure it's safe here?" Jenny asked Maya, worried.

"Don't worry," Maya said soothingly. "Nobody is going to bother us. Isn't that so, Ralph?"

"That's right, the only boogie man around here is me." Ralph turned in his seat and put on a scary face which, for him, didn't take much effort. "*Roooaarrr!*"

Laura let out a loud squeal, shrinking back in her seat. Laughing, Maya pointed to the site farthest away from the lake. "Pete, drive over there. There'll be less chance of getting bitten by midges."

Pete stepped on the gas and steered the Tacoma up to the site. Getting out of the vehicle, Ralph walked around the back and took out the two tents they'd brought with them. One for him and Maya, one for Pete.

He looked at Maya, who'd just got out of the car too. "So, how we going to do this?"

"You and Pete sleep in one tent. I'll sleep in the other with the girls," she replied.

"Fine. So long as you tuck me in and give me my goodnight kiss."

CHAPTER 31

Maya woke up at 7 a.m. She poked her head out the tent flap to see a shimmering mist rising off the lake. Above the tree line, the early morning sun was already intent on burning it off, and it looked to be another sweltering day. She roused everyone from their slumber and soon they all emerged from their tents to join her.

The previous night had passed by uneventfully. While Ralph and Pete pitched the tents, she and Jenny had prepared a simple supper of tinned pork and beans, which they doled out onto plastic plates and eaten with spoons. Soon after, they had all gone to bed.

The two tents had been pitched next to each other, and Ralph took the spot by the entrance to his, the flap unzipped, his Bushmaster next to him, cocked and locked. In Maya's tent, Laura and Jenny whispered to each other in the dark for a while before finally nodding off. Rolling onto her side on the thin foam mattress, Maya had done the same.

The five ate their breakfast unhurriedly. Afterward, they packed the tents and stowed them in the back of the Tacoma, along with the rest of the camping gear.

While Ralph lit up his first cigarette of the day, Pete strolled over to Maya, who leaned over the pickup's hood consulting the map. "Where to, navigator?" he asked, staring over her shoulder.

She pointed a brightly painted fingernail down at the map. "We're here, Toto Creek Park. If we drive north, we can pick up Highway 136 and cross the lake, then head east toward Don Carter State Park. It can't be more than sixty miles away."

"Why there?"

"I have a hunch there'll be survivors there. It's got plenty of forest, and the northern tip of Lake Lanier runs down the entire eastern border. That makes it a good area to fish as well as hunt."

"Sounds good to me. Who knows, maybe our luck will improve today." Pete glanced over at Laura and Jenny. They sat on either side of Ralph at the picnic table while he smoked his cigarette. He smiled. "I'm not sure the girls quite fit into Walter's expectation of 'able-bodied men and women'. They're a bit young for that."

"Don't let Laura hear you say that. She's chuffed that she and Jenny are the camp's very first recruits."

Maya stared across at the bench where Laura leaned against Ralph's shoulder, her golden curls blowing gently in the morning breeze. Since arriving at the park the previous evening, she had stuck to the bank robber like glue, prattling away while he did his chores, handing him the poles and stakes as he and Pete erected the tents. She'd obviously tapped into the same reassuring presence that lurked beneath his ferocious features that Maya first had. Even Jenny, though more reserved, felt it. There was just something about Ralph that made a woman feel safe.

Taking one last drag, Ralph flicked his cigarette into the bushes, then stood. He strolled over to the pickup, Laura and Jenny in tow. "All set?"

Pete nodded. "Time to find some more recruits to add to the party." He winked at the girls. "It won't be easy. We got a certain standard to maintain."

"What we need is a couple of gun-toting Christians to add to the mix. God-fearing people we can trust," Ralph said. "Maybe we can even get a prayer meeting going in the evenings back at camp," he added with a grin.

Maya chuckled. "Never took you for much of a Christian. Did I miss out on that, somehow?"

"Nope, just that prison taught me to sooner trust a man who knows their Genesis to Revelation than one who doesn't. Just the way it is."

"So long as they shoot straight, I'm game," Pete said, laughing. He clapped his hands. "All right everybody, into the truck. Keep your eyes skinned for anyone with a Bible sticking out of their pack. Pox can't have taken them all away!"

CHAPTER 32

Outside Zephyr House, five people piled into the old Volkswagen station wagon. With Fred's grudging acquiescence, Marcie climbed in stiffly behind the wheel. Even at seventy-three years of age, she was the fittest member of the group to drive the vehicle. Simone came a close second. Judging her by her motorcycling experience, though, Marcie had made it clear she had no intention of letting the fifteen-year-old drive.

Beside her in the front passenger seat sat Fred. Eric had expertly plucked him out of his wheelchair and placed him in the seat, after which Simone had wheeled the chair around to the back of the car and placed it in the trunk.

Marcie started the engine, released the handbrake, and drove up the drive, where at the gate, Billy jumped out and opened it. After she passed through, he closed it again and jumped back in beside Eric, with Simone sitting over at the far window.

Twenty minutes later, they reached the junction of Clarks Bridge Road and headed north in the direction of Clermont. Driving parallel to the Don Carter State Park a few miles to their east, they continued north until they reached Nopone Road and turned left onto it.

After driving half a mile, Billy leaned forward and tapped Marcie lightly on the shoulder. "Take this turn here," he said, pointing to a narrow country road coming up on their right. "It's the shortcut to the farm."

Slowing down, Marcie glanced up at the rearview mirror with a frown. "There's another car behind us," she said. "You think it's been following us?"

Fred swiveled in his seat. So did Simone, and caught a glimpse of a pickup truck about five hundred yards back. It disappeared from view as Marcie made the turn.

"I didn't see it," Fred said anxiously. "Did you catch the color or make?"

"It was a dark brown pickup," Simone replied. "I couldn't make out the model."

"Dammit. The men who attacked us three days ago drove a brown Dodge Ram."

Simone stared at him in alarm. "You think they followed us from the house?"

"I don't know. Let's hope not. Marcie, put your foot down. We'll find out soon enough."

The road ran in a straight line for about a mile. Marcie stepped on the accelerator and the Volkswagen slowly picked up speed. Other than her and Eric, all eyes stared anxiously out the back window.

Ten seconds later, behind them, a brown pickup came around the corner. It picked up speed, quickly gaining ground.

"It's them!" Fred groaned, his neck craned at an awkward angle as he stared out the back window. Turning back in his seat, he grabbed his Savage-Steven 12 gauge shotgun resting between his knees. "Get ready for trouble. Looks like they mean business."

Simone reached into her pocket and withdrew her Glock. Billy buzzed down his window, then grabbed his Remington resting on the back ledge.

"No, Billy!" Simone cried out. "You're too young to get involved in this."

"I'm only three years younger than you," Billy told her firmly. "And I *am* involved in this."

"Fred, what do you think?" Simone asked uncertainly.

Fred stuck the barrel of his shotgun out the window. He glanced back briefly. "If they start shooting, we'll need all the firepower we can muster," he said grimly.

"Is there anything I can do?" Eric asked anxiously, his tall frame sitting awkwardly between Simone and Billy.

"Keep your head down and stay alive," Fred told him. "Without you, I'm no good to anybody."

The pickup continued to draw closer. Simone could make out it was a late model Dodge Ram. It was obvious they weren't going to outrun it.

A long burst of gunfire erupted from behind them. "Get down!" Fred yelled.

"My God, that sounded like rifle fire," Eric said, ducking his head. To either side of him, Simone and Billy did likewise. "Last time they only had pistols."

"Yeah," Fred replied tersely. "Looks like they've been to a gun store since then."

The next bend loomed ahead. Marcie kept going at full speed as another heavy stream of gunfire opened up. Bullets slammed into the Volkswagen's bodywork. Several holes appeared in the back window, each one surrounded by a spider's web of cracked glass.

"Bastards!" Fred yelled furiously. He leaned his head out the window, took aim, and fired off two shots. No appreciable damage appeared on the pursuing vehicle.

"Too far away for a shotgun," he muttered. He clicked open the breach, ejected both casings, and reloaded the weapon.

Simone leaned out her window and popped off several shots from her Glock. At least one bullet found its mark. The pickup's front windshield shattered on the driver side and it immediately slowed down.

"Good shooting!" Fred shouted gleefully. "That'll make them think twice about what they're getting into."

Simone knew the relief was only temporary. Armed with semi-automatic rifles against their shotguns and pistols, she doubted the men would give up that easily.

A moment later, Marcie took the bend. The Volkswagen's wheels skidded dangerously in the dirt of the road's margin just as the shooting up started again.

As it straightened out, the car slowed down. Simone spun around in her seat. "Marcie, keep going!" she yelled in dismay.

Marcie clutched the steering wheel, her arms ramrod straight, staring fixedly ahead. "My God, it's a trap!" she screamed.

Simone stared out the windscreen. Five hundred yards away, a blue pickup truck bore down on them. A rifle poked out of the front passenger window, pointing straight at them.

"How the hell…" Fred exclaimed in disbelief.

"Damned if I know." A determined look came over Marcie's face. She hunched over the wheel, steered the Volkswagen into the middle of the road and drove down the white line. "Time to play a game of chicken. Let's see who blinks first."

CHAPTER 33

Leaving Toto Creek Park behind them, Ralph and his group had made good progress over the past hour. Pete had picked up Highway 136 and driven east through north-central Georgia. Maintaining a steady seventy, they'd put on the miles in smart order. When they reached the junction of State Route 283, they swung north onto it, and after a couple more miles, crossed Lake Lanier over the Wahoo Creek Bridge.

A short time later, Maya instructed Pete to turn right onto a secondary road, and they drove eastward once more. "We're only fifteen miles away from the park," she said, consulting the map. "Should be there soon."

The scenery to either side of the road was beautiful, comprised of lush meadows, rolling hills, and gently sloping valleys, interspersed by forests and lakes. They passed several large estates with high-end mansions perched on the tops of hills with huge gardens and fancy stone pillar gates.

"Looks like there used to be money here before the shit hit the fan," Pete commented. "How about we take one of these back roads and check out some of these farms I've seen signposted?"

"No harm in taking a look," Maya replied.

At the next junction, Pete swung onto a narrow country lane where a mixture of forest and agricultural land lay to either side of the road.

After a couple of miles, Ralph turned in his seat. "All right girls, remember our mission. Keep your eyes peeled for any signs of life, okay?"

"What kind of life?" Laura asked. "Do you mean humans, or animals too?"

"Anything. If there are any animals still alive, most likely there'll be people nearby too. You see as much as a skinny little dog on its own, you holler out."

Laura's eyes darted past Ralph's, staring out through the windscreen. "Ralph, I'm hollering!" she shouted excitedly. "It's not a skinny dog either…look!"

Ralph spun back around in his seat. A few hundred yards ahead of them, traveling at speed, an old gray station wagon swung around the bend, barely holding the road.

The sound of gunfire erupted. "Are they shooting at us?" Pete asked incredulously.

"No idea." Ralph grabbed his Bushmaster. Switching the rifle's safety position from *safe* to *fire*, he thrust the barrel out the window. "Watch out people. Looks like trouble coming our way."

As if to confirm his suspicions, the station wagon suddenly pulled out into the middle of the road, refusing to make any room for the approaching Tacoma.

"Sweet Jesus!" Pete screamed in alarm. He tugged hard at the wheel and swerved across to the hard shoulder, skidding to a stop.

Moments later, the station wagon shot past them. Ralph caught sight of a gray-haired lady hunched behind the wheel. Beside her sat an old man of similar age. Sticking out his window was a rifle of some description.

As the vehicle flashed by, Ralph saw that three distinct bullet holes peppered the rear window. Before he had time to think, a brown pickup truck hurtled around the bend, driving even faster than the station wagon. Its windscreen was broken, a large hole punched out where the driver's face stared grimly out. Rifle barrels stuck out all three passenger windows.

"What the f—" Ralph exclaimed as the vehicle drove past. The four men inside barely glanced at them. One leaned his head out the window. Aiming his rifle clumsily, he opened up on the station wagon, and the sound of gunfire broke out again. At that distance and without proper sighting, Ralph doubted he'd hit the vehicle.

"What on Earth is going on?" Pete asked, a bewildered look on his face. "Those guys look hellbent on killing that old couple."

"Beats me," Ralph replied tersely.

"I saw a girl in the back of the first car," Jenny said. Sitting on the side facing the road, she'd had a better view than Ralph. "A black girl about my age."

"Should we help them?" Maya asked worriedly. "We've got two children to think of."

"We should help," Jenny said. "Just like you helped us." She looked over at her friend.

"Do it," Laura said firmly.

"You hear the ladies," Ralph told Pete. "Do it."

Without a word, Pete pulled hard on the wheel and drove the Taco back onto the road. Making a three point turn, he floored the gas pedal and took off after the two vehicles.

"Okay girls. The two of you need to crouch down behind the seats," Ralph instructed. "Maya, make sure they keep their heads down, yours as well."

"Ralph, is this going to be a car chase like you see in the movies?" Laura asked excitedly.

"That's right, little doll. Now do as you're told and get your head down. Things might get a tad frisky."

***

The Dodge Ram gained distance on them once more. Simone leaned over the back ledge and knocked out a large hole in the rear window with the butt of her gun. It was harder than she thought, the laminated glass was tough to break through.

Marcie glanced at her in the mirror. "Simone, get down! They'll start firing again any second!"

Now that she'd made herself a better position to shoot from, Simone ducked down behind her seat again. Peeking over the ledge, she stared out the hole and saw that the blue pickup had turned around to join the chase and was gaining ground fast. "Their friends are following us now too!" she yelled.

She flinched and ducked her head as another burst of gunfire opened up and several rounds pinged off the Volkswagen's bodywork. Lifting her head, she aimed her Glock through the hole and released several single-spaced shots. Whether she hit the vehicle or not she had no idea, but unlike last time, her shooting made no difference and the Ram continued to speed toward them.

Behind the Ram, the blue pickup opened fire. *Idiots*, Simone thought to herself. *They're going to hit their own men if they're not careful.*

Sure enough, after another burst of gunfire, the Ram started to swerve from side to side. In the next moment, it lost control and careened off the road and into a patch of rough grass.

Disbelieving, Simone watched as whoever was handling the rifle in the blue pickup continued to fire at it as they sped by.

"Hey!" she shouted. "The new people are firing at the other guys, not us!"

It only occurred to her then how unlikely it was that the men in the blue pickup had anything to do with those in the Ram. They couldn't possibly have known that Marcie would take the shortcut Billy had led her down. In the heat of the moment, no one had had time to think properly.

"You sure?" Marcie asked, staring anxiously in the rearview mirror. Concentrating on her driving, she obviously hadn't seen the Ram being forced off the road.

"Positive." The blue pickup continued to bear down on them, then its headlights began flashing. "Marcie, stop! They want to talk to us."

Marcie glanced in her mirror again, her foot flat on the pedal as another straight stretch of road opened up in front of them.

"Stop, dammit!" Fred yelled at her. "Whoever they are, they're on our side."

Marcie took her foot off the pedal and applied it to the brakes. The Volkswagen slowed down and after another seventy yards, she pulled over to the side of the road. The blue pickup slowed too. Moments later, it glided to a stop beside them.

A large man with jet black hair and a horribly disfigured face leaned his head out the front passenger window. Draped over the frame, on his right hand was a large skull ring with sinister ruby eyes. For one awful moment, Simone thought she'd made a terrible mistake. Perhaps these people weren't friends after all.

"What the hell do you mean by running us off the road like that?" the man growled fiercely at Marcie. Then he looked over at Fred and broke out into a big grin. "Mister, you always let your old lady drive like that? She's going to get you killed one of these days."

CHAPTER 34

Fifteen minutes later, ten people sat or stood around the kitchen table at Willow Spring Farm, acquainting each other with their tales of survival. Back on the road earlier, after a brief discussion, Pete had followed the battered station wagon back to the farm where, on arrival, a young boy had brought everyone into the kitchen.

"So all five of you intend on living here, is that the plan?" Maya asked Fred, who sat in his wheelchair at the top of the table. He and Marcie had done most of the talking for their group.

"That's right. It's got everything we need. Seeing as Billy was born and raised here, he knows everything there is to know about running the place, right, Billy?"

"Most things," the young boy replied solemnly. "Not everything."

"Well, what you don't know, Marcie can teach you. She's a farmer too."

"Really?" Maya said, staring at Marcie curiously. "That's a useful profession these days."

"Before I got married, I was a nurse. That's a useful profession too," Marcie told her. "As for the farm, we grew mainly cereals. Still, between the five of us, we'll figure it out." She looked over at Ralph and Pete, who stood leaning against the back wall. "You say your camp is in the Cohutta. That's a good four hour drive away. What exactly brings you here?"

"We're on a recruitment hunt," Pete explained. "We've established a camp with plenty of good land. We're just short people to help run it."

"Why, how many of you are there?"

Pete gestured over at Laura and Jenny who sat at one corner of the table. "Including our first two recruits, we number ten in total."

Marcie smiled at the girls. "Looks like you got off to a good start."

Laura stared back at her. "Marcie, do you read the Bible?" she asked hesitantly.

"Uh…it's been a while," Marcie replied, looking a little confused.

"How about you, Fred?"

"Not since I was about your age. Why?"

Laughing, Maya explained. "This morning, Ralph suggested we should find some God-fearing Christians to join us. I think Laura was hoping that might be you guys."

"Sorry to disappoint you," Marcie said, chuckling. "Though perhaps it's just as well, seeing as we don't have any intention of leaving here. All of us are excited to help Billy run this place."

"Aren't you worried about defending it by yourselves?" Pete asked. "No offense, but you guys are kind of vulnerable. What if the gang that just attacked you finds this place? You say you think they're from around here somewhere."

"Don't worry. Once we get settled in, we'll keep those ruffians at bay," Fred said confidently. "Appreciate your concern, but we'll do just fine."

Ralph was doubtful. "Then you'll need to get yourself better weapons. It's hard to defend against semi-automatic rifles with shotguns and pistols."

"You're right," Simone said. She looked at him. "What do you suggest we get?"

"Any type of AR-15 is best. Make sure they're chambered in 5.56mm. There's more availability—"

He flinched as a volley of gunfire erupted outside. At the front of the house, there was the sound of glass breaking.

"What the hell!" Fred exclaimed.

Ralph snatched his Bushmaster leaning against the kitchen cabinets. "Come on, Pete!" he yelled, running over to the hall door. "Everyone else, stay here."

"We'll watch the garden!" Fred shouted after him, wheeling himself over to where he'd left his shotgun. "Make sure no one come around the back and surprises us."

Ralph raced down the hall with Pete following right behind him. He ducked into the living room and over to the window. Both panes were broken, and a pile of glass lay on the floor.

He poked his head cautiously around the curtains and stared up the driveway. At the gates, two men stood to one side of the pillars. Parked next to them, the rear bumper of a brown pickup truck could be seen. "Damn, they followed us here," he cursed under his breath.

Pete stepped out and darted across the window to the far side, his AR-15 clutched in his hands. Immediately, a fusillade of gunfire opened up, bullets thudding into the back wall behind him.

"That was close!" Pete gasped.

"Pete, watch how I do this," Ralph said. "Less chance of getting hit."

He poked the muzzle of the Bushmaster out the window. Peeking just one eye around the window frame, he aimed the rifle at the top of the driveway and opened fire. Pete followed suit, and soon the harsh sound of gunfire echoed around the room.

The two attackers ducked behind the pillar. There was the sound of doors slamming, and then an engine starting.

Next moment, the pickup jerked forward and disappeared from view.

Pete lowered his rifle with a relieved grin. "Didn't seem like they wanted to put up much of a fight, did they?"

"For now. They'll be back, though," Ralph replied. "Pete, you need to persuade these folk to come back to Eastwood with us. No way in hell can we let them stay here. They won't last a week."

Pete frowned. "You heard them. They're determined to live here. How can I get them to change their minds?"

"I don't know. Sell them on how great our camp is. How for a limited time only, all blind people, invalids, and grannies are welcome. But they got to hurry, the offer ends tonight." Ralph headed for the door. "Come on, stop looking like a gormless douche and get ready to hustle!"

CHAPTER 35

The following day, Walter set out from Camp Eastwood in his Tundra. Cody rode shotgun, the stock of his Ruger SR-556 carbine jammed between his knees, barrel pointing out the window.

It had been almost a week since the group left Wasson Lodge. Walter wanted to meet with Sheriff Rollins and let him know that he hadn't reneged on his promise to build him his micro hydro. It was something he had intended to do sooner, but had delayed until Pete, Ralph, and Maya returned from their recruitment mission. He'd had no intention of leaving their new camp while they were gone, undermining its defenses even further.

"How are you and Emma getting on?" he asked, steering the pickup down the dirt and gravel road. "Still at that lovey dovey, touchy feely stage?"

Cody felt his cheeks reddening. Over the course of the past few days, he and Emma had spent every moment of their free time together, either in Cody's trailer making love, or out exploring the Cohutta wilderness where there was a certain rock pool they liked to frequent. "I guess," he replied embarrassedly. "Sometimes, I think maybe it's a little weird given the times we're in. All this death and destruction around us."

Walter shook his head. "Not at all. Make the most of it. *Particularly* because of the times we're in."

Cody laughed. "All right. Will do." He changed the topic. "I took Simone and Marcie out for target practice this morning. They're both pretty good shots. And Fred's not bad either. With Eric pushing him around the place, the two make one heck of a good defender."

Walter chuckled. "Pete will be relieved to hear that. The expression on his face when he got back yesterday was priceless. Haven't seen him look that mortified since the time he showed up with Mason at the Chevron station."

On their return to camp the previous evening, an uncomfortable-looking Pete had introduced the seven new recruits. Everyone had struggled to keep the astonishment off their faces: two seventy-year-olds, one of them wheelchair bound, a blind man, and a gaggle of children hadn't quite been what anyone had been expecting him to return with. Pete insisted it had taken some persuasion on his part to get them to come, too.

"Billy brought plenty to get the farm going," Cody said. "That's going to help."

As well as the human additions, the group had towed back two twelve-foot trailers containing a variety of farm animals, plants, seeds, and farming equipment, including two hoop tunnels, rabbit hutches, and a chicken tractor. It boded well for their move down to the valley.

He glanced at Walter. "Billy says he's good with a gun as well. Told me his father taught him how to use one when he was ten years old. I'm not sure whether to believe him or not."

Walter remained silent a while before speaking. "Normally I wouldn't weapons train a twelve-year-old boy for defense purposes. It's not right. But times have changed. If need be, it's better Billy defends the camp than let it fall victim to bandits. Especially seeing as we've got several young girls to take care of now."

"All right. Tomorrow, I'll take him up to the range. My father taught me to shoot at his age, too. 'Course, that was a little different. He trained me to shoot deer, not people."

They crossed Jacks River over the concrete bridge dividing Georgia from Tennessee, and headed up Peavine Road. It took almost a straight line due north, connecting with Baker Creek Road, and took them past the Harris Branch where Cody had gone hunting with Eddy a week ago. With all that had occurred since, it felt far longer than that.

Thirty minutes later, they swung around a long bend and Lake Ocoee's clear blue waters came into view. Soon they turned onto Cookson Creek Road and passed Devil's Point. Minutes later, the turn for Wasson Lodge came up on their right.

Walter peered through the windscreen and frowned. "Looks like the sheriff took down the checkpoint. That's not good."

"You don't think Chris has fallen out with him, do you?" Cody asked, staring out the window. With a depleted group at the lodge, it made even more sense for the checkpoint to remain in operation.

Walter shrugged. "It's possible. Chris is the sort who'd start a fight in an empty bar."

Passing the turn, Cody stared out his side window. He spotted an unfamiliar pickup truck parked across the driveway, blocking the entrance. Two strangers sat in the bed, the barrels of their rifles sticking out over the panel. Both men stared at the passing Tundra with hostile expressions.

"Looks like Chris has found some new recruits as well. Can't say they look too friendly," Walter remarked.

They arrived at the turn for Camp Benton, where both men noted that the South Cookson checkpoint had also been removed. Walter tugged at the wheel and turned into the entranceway.

Two hundred yards ahead, an eight-wheeler flatbed truck sat parked across the road. To either side, trees had been felled, preventing any vehicle from driving around it.

"Looks like they moved the checkpoint here," Cody said, staring up the forested drive.

As they got closer, they saw that sandbags had been stacked two-high along the truck bed. Three men stood behind them, their rifles pointing outward. One raised his in the air and two shots rang out in quick succession. Immediately, he lowered his rifle again and trained it on the oncoming Tundra.

"What the hell!" Walter exclaimed, jamming his foot on the brakes.

Out of the corner of his eye, Cody saw movement in the woods to his left. A figure stood behind a tree, aiming his rifle at the driver-side window.

Walter spotted him too. "Don't move a muscle," he said out of the corner of his mouth, his head motionless. "Not even a twitch."

Cody had absolutely no intention of doing so. He sat ramrod straight, staring ahead. Slowly, Walter reached his hand over to the driver door and buzzed down his window. "Don't shoot!" he yelled. "We're here to see Sheriff Rollins."

The figure stepped out from behind the tree and walked over to them, his AR-15 held level in his grip. When he got closer, Walter breathed a sigh of relief. "Sam, that you? It's me…Walter!" He turned to Cody. "It's all right, I know Sam."

The man was unfamiliar to Cody who, unlike Walter, hadn't spent much time at Camp Benton. "Just hope he hasn't forgotten you," he replied, feeling some of the tension leaving his body.

As the guard reached the pickup, he waved over to his companions, gesturing for them to lower their weapons.

"Dammit, Sam," Walter said, shaking his head. "You guys are kind of jumpy, ain't you? Looked like you were about to open up on us."

"If you'd gotten any closer, we would have. Everyone is a little skittish right now." Though friendly, there was a tense look on Sam's face as he spoke.

"So I see. What the hell is going on?"

Sam scratched the side of his head. "We've had trouble lately. Plenty of it. Three of our men got murdered the other day. They took Ned Granger hostage. We only managed to free him yesterday."

"Oh man. I'm sorry to hear that."

Sam stared at Walter. "I'm guessing you haven't heard the news about the lodge either, have you?"

"No. What news?"

"Same bandits that killed our men stormed it a couple of nights ago. They killed Chris and the rest of the men." Sam pointed a finger back toward the junction. "Following morning, bastards dumped their bodies at the top of our driveway. We had to bury them ourselves."

Walter turned to face Cody, aghast. Cody stared back. The dismantling of the Cookson Road checkpoints and the strangers in the lodge's driveway all made sense now.

"Liz got away," Sam continued. "She ran straight here that night. That's how we know all the details."

"I can't believe it," Walter barely managed to stutter out. "Are you telling me that Liz is the only Camp Knox member to survive?"

Sam nodded grimly. "Now you know what has us so edgy. We've got an enemy living a mile from our camp who's murdered seven people."

He twirled a finger at the guards behind the eight-wheeler, indicating that they start the engine. "Go on up to the camp. The sheriff will fill you in on the details. It's pretty simple, really. Basically, we're at war."

CHAPTER 36

Walter and Cody sat at the table opposite Sheriff Rollins. The sheriff had waited at the graveled lot at the top of the driveway to greet the two men when they stepped out of their vehicle, then escorted them down to the main square. Sam had obviously radioed ahead from the checkpoint to inform him of their arrival.

Though his manner was cordial, it was plain to see the increased tension in his demeanor since they last met. Taking the two into the cabin that served as the Benton's council room, Rollins recounted everything that had occurred since Walter and his group left Wasson Lodge: the murder of three of his men on a scavenging run to Cleveland where Ned Granger had been taken hostage, how the lodge had been overrun and Chris and three of his men killed, and finally, how Rollins had found out where Granger had been taken prisoner and rescued him.

Having turned the tables on the gang, one of its members was now in custody. If his leader, a man by the name of Mason, didn't vacate Wasson Lodge by the following morning, Rollins intended on executing the prisoner for his crimes. According to both Ned and Liz, he was deeply implicated in all seven murders.

Walter stared at Rollins with a look of incredulity. "The leader's name is Mason? Is he from Knoxville, by any chance?"

Rollins frowned. "That's right. Why, do you know him?"

"Is he real big?" Cody butted in. "Bald, with long straggly hair at the back?"

"That's him." The sheriff leaned forward at the table, his eyes narrowing. "You two need to tell me how come you're acquainted with the sonofabitch who killed three of my men."

"Sheriff, we're from Knoxville too," Walter replied. "We had a run-in with him before we left." He tapped the back of his leg. "Remember the bullet I took in my calf? Well, he's the one that put it there."

"I don't understand. How the hell did he get here?" Cody said with a perplexed expression. "Walter, do you think he followed us when we got away from the gas station that day?"

"No," Walter replied adamantly. "No one followed us through those back streets, I'm certain of it."

"Then how come he's here? Is this just coincidence?"

Rollins stood up from his chair. "I don't know, but we'll get to the bottom of it soon enough." He strode across the room and flung open the door. "Jake!" he called out to someone outside on the square. "Go find Ned. Tell him to bring Russ here. I got some questions for him."

Rollins closed the door and took his seat at the table again. "Russ is the name of our prisoner. He scouted out the area before Mason arrived. That name mean anything to you, Walter?"

"Nope, but if he's part of Mason's outfit, I might recognize him."

The three had to wait several minutes until there was the sound of footsteps outside. A moment later, the door opened and Ned Granger stepped into the room. Using a stick as a cane, he hobbled over to the table and shook

Walter's hand warmly. Both men being Gulf War veterans, it was clear to Cody that the two had previously bonded. Granger shook Cody's hand, then sat down beside Rollins.

"I hope you came back to fulfill your promise, Walter," he said, staring across the table. "Camp Benton still anxiously awaits power. We hauled a couple of freezers here recently so that we can stock up on freshly killed game. Just waiting for you to do your magic." He smiled. "Sure would be nice to read a book in the evenings too."

"That's the reason we came here," Walter assured him. "Of course, that was before we heard the news…"

Just then, the door opened and two men hauled a small, wiry man into the room. Bedraggled-looking, his arms were cuffed behind his back. He looked familiar to Cody, though he couldn't quite place him.

Walter recognized him straightaway. "Yeah, that's one of Mason's men. He was with him at the gas station that day."

Granger's eyebrows shot up. "Wait, you know Mason?" he exclaimed.

"Unfortunately." Walter stared at Russ fiercely. "What the hell are you doing here in the Cohutta?"

A smirk appeared briefly on Russ's face, like he couldn't help himself. "I followed you on my motorbike. You guys didn't spot me, did you?"

Walter's frown deepened. "But how did you find us? You didn't track us down after we left the gas station. I'm sure of it."

"True, but the next day I rode the highways all morning until I caught up with you. You were heading for the Toyota dealership on Parkside Drive. Maybe I got lucky, but with no one on the roads, it wasn't as hard as you might think."

"Then you followed us here to Lake Ocoee, is that it?" Cody asked.

"I had no choice. I would have lost you otherwise. Mason told me not to come back until I knew where you were."

"Are you telling me that Mason came all the way to the Cohutta just to find us?" Walter said incredulously. "That makes no sense at all."

Russ shook his head. "He'd been planning to leave the city for a while. When I told him how good things were here, he decided to come take a look. Catching up with you guys was just the icing on the cake. Of course…everything's changed now." He looked at Granger pleadingly. "Ned, I've told you everything I know about Mason and his plans. That counts for something, right?"

"Sure it does. You didn't get waterboarded, did you? The way you blubbered everything so easily, there'd have been no fun in it." Granger stared at him coldly. "Whether you live or die is a different matter. That's up to Mason." He nodded at the two guards. "Take him back to his room. I can't bear the sight of him a moment longer."

The two guards seized Russ by each arm and dragged him out of the room.

Cody stole a glance at Walter, who sat stiffly at the table beside him, the muscles in his face twitching as he grasped the enormity of the situation. Unwittingly, they had been the conduit by which Mason and his gang had come to the Cohutta.

Gathering his resolve, Walter looked Rollins in the eye. "Sheriff, as you heard from Russ, we had no idea Mason followed us here." He glanced briefly at Cody. "Still, I know I speak for both of us when I say how terrible we feel about what has happened. We owe you and all at Camp Benton an apology."

"Absolutely," Cody murmured.

"Thank you both." Rollins said. "I can't possibly blame you that Mason followed you here. It was just bad luck."

"Bad luck that Mason survived vPox. Of all the people…" Granger added grimly. "But like John says, it wasn't your fault he turned up here."

Walter looked relieved.

"So what happens now?" Cody asked. "At the checkpoint, Sam said you're at war. That true?"

"Depends on Mason," Rollins replied. "I've given him an ultimatum to vacate the lodge by tomorrow morning or we'll execute Russ. Somehow, I doubt that threat is enough to persuade him to leave."

"I doubt it either," Granger said.

Rollins stared at Walter and Cody. "The execution is scheduled for 9 a.m. tomorrow morning. You should both stay the night. I think it's fitting you witness it as a tribute to those who have been murdered."

"We'll stay," Walter said, firmly. "It's the least we can do."

CHAPTER 37

The next morning at 8:45 a.m., Rollins made the call. Sitting at the staffroom table, he picked up the radio keyed into Wasson Lodge and jabbed the Push button. Beside him at the table was Ned Granger.

"Mason, this is Sheriff Rollins. Do you read me? Over."

A moment later, Mason's sour voice came over the channel. *"Yeah, Rollins. I hear you. What do you want?"*

"Time to make your decision. If you want Russ's life spared, you need to vacate the lodge right away. What is it to be? Over."

There was no hesitation in Mason's reply. *"Fuck you. I ain't leaving. Matter of fact, in the next couple of days, I'm going to be standing right where you are now, with my boot on your head."*

"Dream on, Mason. You got less than twenty men, not sixty. No way in hell will you take this place, over."

"We'll see about that. Either way, I'm staying."

"Your choice. You got any last message for Russ? Over."

"What's there to say? Tell him that's how war goes. Over and out."

The radio went dead. With a shrug, Rollins placed the handset back down on the table. "Just like we thought, Ned.

This thing isn't over yet. All right, I'll find Mary and the others. You go fetch Russ."

Granger stood up from the table. "See you at the beach in fifteen. Time to rid the world of this weasel."

***

Russ Willis lay on the bed in the cabin that served as his cell. His right hand dangled over the side where it was cuffed to a three-quarter inch steel chain that had been looped through a concrete hollow block. His ankles were chained too, in a set of leg irons courtesy of Benton's sheriff's department. Ned Granger wasn't taking any chances.

He checked his watch. 8:50 a.m. The relentless feeling of terror he'd felt these past thirty-six hours burrowed deeper into his stomach. He prayed he wouldn't die that day, but knew that the situation was out of his control. No amount of cunning would save him now. It was up to Mason.

At the crack of dawn that morning, his heart had lifted momentarily. He'd heard gunshots close by. His optimism was short-lived, however. After less than thirty seconds of intense gunfire, the shooting stopped again. It appeared that Mason's attempt to break into the camp had been unsuccessful.

But surely his friend wouldn't forsake him, he reasoned, and would acquiesce to the sheriff's demands. Russ's cunning and guile was worth more to Mason than the lodge, right? After all, there were plenty of other places they could move on to. The world was full of them.

He heard footsteps coming up the porch steps. A key turned in the lock and the door swung open. Light streamed into the room, causing him to blink momentarily at a figure standing in the doorway, one that after a couple more blinks he recognized.

"Get up, Russ," Ned Granger said in a quiet voice. "It's time."

He stepped into the room, followed by two more men who came over to the bed. One bent over and undid his manacles, while the other released him from the leg cuffs. Grasping him by each arm, they pulled him off the bed and up to his feet.

Russ stared at Granger. "Ned, did the sheriff talk to Mason?" he asked, so terrified he could barely get the words out.

"Yeah, "Granger replied.

"Wh-what did he say?"

"He said he couldn't live without you, of course. He's packing his bags as we speak, ready to head back to Knoxville. The limo should be here to collect you any moment."

Standing to either side of Russ, both guards sniggered.

"*No...*" Russ moaned as reality sunk in. His legs buckled as the last vestiges of his dignity deserted him. He sank to his knees and threw himself down at Granger's feet. "Please, Ned," he sobbed. "I'll do anything...just let me live."

Granger stepped back from him. "Get up, you piece of scum," he grated. "Try and make the last few minutes of your life count for something."

Try as he might, Russ couldn't rise. His strength had left him and he flopped about on the floor like a jellyfish, blubbering incoherently.

Granger nodded to the guards and they dragged him back up to his feet, then Granger turned around and limped out of the cabin on his stick. Clutching him tightly, the two guards frog-marched Russ out of the room, down the wooden steps, and across the short grass after Granger.

They took him in the direction of the lake. A procession of men and women followed, grim expressions on their faces. At the back, he spotted Walter and his friend.

One of the group, a tall young man drew abreast of him. Russ recognized him as one of the men who'd rescued Granger two days ago.

"You killed my friends, you sick bastard," he hissed. "Now we're going to send you to Hell, where you belong."

"Easy, Kit," Granger said softly. He stopped a few yards ahead and turned around. "Let's do this the right way."

With one last glance, the young man spun away angrily and rejoined his companions.

The group passed along a trail through the forest. A few minutes later, they reached a small cove, where a twelve-foot post had been erected ten yards from the lake shore. Seeing it, Russ's legs gave way again. The two guards gripped his arms even tighter and dragged him over to it.

When they reached the post, one of the men bent over and grabbed a length of rope that had been left coiled on the ground beside it. The second guard spun Russ around and pressed his back up against the post.

Starting at his feet, the first man looped the rope tightly around his ankles, securing them to the post. Making his way up, he soon wrapped the rope around Russ's chest and under his arms. A few final loops were made around his neck to hold his head in place, and it was done.

Four men separated from the watching group, all carrying rifles. One of them was the young man named Kit. Sheriff Rollins and Ned Granger walked over to stand beside them.

"Russ Willis," the sheriff called out in a loud voice, "as a proven murderer of three brave members of the Benton Survivors Group— Marcus Welby, Joe Macey, and Bob Harper—as well as four members of the Fort Knox Group, the council of Benton hereby condemns you to death by firing squad. Is there anything you wish to say before your execution?"

Russ was incapable of answering. He couldn't believe what was happening. Was he really about to die? He scanned the rocks to either side of the cove, desperately hoping that this would be the moment when Mason made his move to attack the camp, but there was nothing to be seen other than rocks, trees, and brush.

"I said, is there anything you wish to say before your execution?" Rollins repeated.

"No," Russ whimpered. His bladder opened up, and a warm river gushed down his leg. He felt no shame, though. Fear had totally overwhelmed his sense of ignominy.

"Very well."

Rollins made a gesture to the remaining guard still standing beside Russ, who produced a white pillowcase from somewhere. Raising it, he yanked it over Russ's head, and the last thing he saw of the world was the four-man firing squad as they each bent down on one knee.

The guard pressed his mouth up against his ear. "Enjoy Hell, motherfucker," he whispered, before stepping away.

There was the sound of rifles being released off their safeties.

"*Ready…*"

Was this really happening? This wasn't supposed to be.

"*Aim…*"

Russ let out one final whimper.

"*Fire!*"

He felt no pain as four fifty-five grain full-metal-jacket rounds ripped into his chest, instantly eviscerating his aorta into chunks of bloodied meat.

His head slumped forward and the light faded from his eyes. Everything went black, and he felt an indefinable essence of his being get sucked down to a dark, eternal place.

FROM THE AUTHOR

For sneak peaks, updates on new releases and bonus content, subscribe to my mailing list at www.mikesheridanbooks.com.

ON THE EDGE, Book 3 in the NO DIRECTION HOME series is out August 2017.

40854648R00117

Printed in Poland
by Amazon Fulfillment
Poland Sp. z o.o., Wrocław